THE FALLEN
IN Soura Heights

AMANDA JAEGER

This book is a work of fiction. All names, characters, locations, and incidents are products of the author's imagination. Any resemblance to actual persons, things, living or dead, locales, or events is entirely coincidental.

Editor: Genevieve A. Scholl
Cover Design: Troy Cooper
Formatted by: Genevieve A. Scholl

TABLE OF CONTENTS

To all who are learning to find themselves.
May you learn the true meaning of strength.

PROLOGUE

"Come on. I'll show you." She opened the car door and offered Jonny Schniber the passenger seat. "It'll just take a few minutes and you'll see."

He climbed into the seat next to her, his head shaking. "Sure, I'll come along for the ride, but I don't think you see the big picture."

She knew he didn't understand. Not yet, anyway. But she was going to change that. She was going to prove to him that things were perfect just the way they were now, as they had always been. Her eyes fixed on the road in front of them, determined to make him understand.

"See, it's been a long time… years even since we've had new families move in. This town has been full of the same people ever since I've been here. I'm sure it's the same for you, too." Was he looking to her for confirmation?

"It doesn't matter, Jonny. We work well just as we are. I like the town quiet and happy. Open up the gates, and you'll see what kind of people could invite themselves here. It would be chaos, Jonny. Absolute chaos. We don't need that. We need consistency, and the only way to have that consistency is to keep it just as it is now."

Jonny sighed and shrugged his shoulders. "I know you like things as they are now, but change has to happen at some point. Nothing ever stays the same forever. We have to grow to save this place. More homes means more families. More business means more jobs. More jobs means more money for all of us."

And more corruption. Doesn't he get that?

The little car pulled into the Covista Forest parking lot. Directly in front of them was a blue sign reading, **Stay on the Path**. The blue path was the most direct hiking trail; barely a hike at all, making a semi-circle around to the other side of the parking lot. It was the path most people took when they wanted fresh air, but it wasn't the one she had in mind.

"Come on." She turned off the ignition. "I'll show you one of my favorite places to be."

Their feet noisily landed among the dirt and gravel as they let themselves out. "You do know that when I make the call, this isn't what I'll be talking about, right? I have no plans to pave over the forest." He sounded so sure of himself.

She hung her head. "Not yet, Jonny. But you start in one place and before you know it, you're choppin' down the trees and chippin' away at what belongs here. You already know where you want to start, but I want to show you where you'll end up."

Together, they followed the blue trail, keeping to the signs until they hit another opening. There, a red sign read, **Keep on the Path**, with an arrow pointing in a new direction. This was a whole new path that was far less direct. It weaved in and around the brush. It twisted and turned. If you walked from this point to the exit, it would take two hours to return to the blue trail. But it was worth it. There was more wildlife to witness, more creeks to enjoy, and once in a while, the sunlight peeked through the canopy in a way that made it feel like you were standing in the middle of a painting.

"The red path?" Jonny huffed. "You want to take the long way around?"

"It's the only way to go, as far as I'm concerned. It's peaceful. It's exactly what I love about Soura Heights."

He sighed. "Okay, let's go. But like I said, I won't be paving over the forest. That's just insanity."

"It's insanity to pave over anythin'. It's literally askin' for trouble."

They continued walking along the red path, watching squirrels scamper and birds twit from tree to tree. She pointed out the creek when they reached it and sat criss-cross on the ground in front of it.

"Sometimes, I come here just to think." She patted the ground next to her. He sat down, too. "All of Soura is just like this spot. It makes me feel... I don't know... happy, I guess. Sitting here, I know that no matter what the rest of the world decides to do to itself, they can't take this away from me." She looked at him, full of hope. If he could only feel it, too, he wouldn't make those plans. He wouldn't make the call to have someone come in and pave over beautiful Soura Heights. He wouldn't destroy what she had always loved.

He shook his head. "Like I said, though, this wouldn't be touched." He stood up from the spot and offered his hand. "Come on. Let's get out of here. I'll show you where I want to put in a new shopping center."

"Jonny, a shoppin' center?" She hoisted herself up without his help and spoke with disdain. "I thought you were going to build new homes!"

"Well yeah, new homes come first, but then we will need a shopping center, too. Busy Street won't be big enough as is. We will need places for people to work, spend their money, maybe even places for tourists to visit."

"Tourists?! The hell, Jonny?" With both hands, she shoved his shoulders away from her. "What the hell are you turnin' this place into?"

He stumbled backward at the second shove, almost tripping over a fallen branch. "Wait a minute. I don't think you understand." He held up both hands in a defensive stance.

"No; *you* don't understand!" She gave him another push. "You want to destroy everythin' that makes this place special and happy. You want to wash it away and clear it out." Another push sent him to the ground. She knelt down in front of him and leaned over his body. "You want to take it all away."

"No, no, wait!" Jonny's voice rose in his throat. He tried to scramble away from her, but she had pinned down his legs by sitting on them. Sweat pooled on his forehead, but she ignored his discomfort. She needed to get through to him, no matter what it took.

Almost in slow motion, she raised her hands over her head and shouted, "I won't let you do it!" Her fists came down hard, hitting him in the temple. "You can't take it away!" She threw her fists down at him again.

She continued to yell, throwing punches at every syllable. Her eyes welled with emotion. She wouldn't allow anyone to take away

11

what she loved—a place full of people who kept quiet and cared for each other more than themselves.

Jonny didn't move. He lay still on the forest floor. But all she saw was the face of the man who was going to change everything. And the more she thought of it, the angrier she became.

When her emotions were finally still, she inhaled deeply. If Jonny didn't understand the importance of keeping Soura Heights the way it had always been, he sure understood now. She climbed off him and offered her hand the same way he had offered his. "Come on. I think you get it, now."

But he didn't move. His body was still.

"Come on, I said!" She forced her stiff hand out again, as if the harder she held it out in front of her, the more enticing it would be for him to stand up.

"Jonny. Stop playin'. You need to get up."

Still nothing.

She knelt down next to him and lifted his arm. She pulled it up. "God, what am I gonna tell Louise, huh? That her husband was late for dinner because he decided to goof off in the forest?"

His hand went limp, landing next to the rest of his body in the dirt.

"Seriously. Get up, Jonny."

For the first time, with clear, unangry eyes, she saw his face. It looked back at her blankly as his head lay on its side, splattered in blood.

Blood? I didn't hit him that hard.

"Jonny?" She lifted his head. On the other side was a rock, covered in blood. She didn't cause any noticeable wound where her hands hit, but there was a clear laceration to his temple where he hit the rock.

"Jonny?" she called again. "Jonny. Get up. Come on." She shook his head, but nothing happened.

Shocked, she let go and watched him lay expressionless on the forest floor.

On all fours, she backed up until she hit a tree trunk. She clasped her hand over her mouth.

He fell. Jonny fell. He fell and hurt himself. That's what happened. That's what had to happen.

Then, she stood herself up. She took in the sight in front of her and drank in its implications.

That's what had to happen for Soura Heights to stay safe.

CHAPTER ONE

Present Day

Fey Anderson felt as if a vise was tightening around her chest. Standing in front of the display window of Tell Me Wear, she couldn't breathe. In front of her was a happy little mannequin family in matching outfits, mocking her panic.

Come on, Fey. Not now. Not again.

The mannequin man's white polo shook before her eyes.

No. It's not shaking. I am.

No; not a mannequin. Her dead husband's face stared back at her, a translucent version no one else could see.

Bruce!

How she missed his face, that five o'clock shadow, that smile that belonged to her. She tried grabbing at it, wishing she could hold onto him once more, but it was no use. Something ... no ... *someone* had taken it from her.

She braced herself on the window and felt heat rise from her chest to her ears. Her chest moved up and down rapidly and even though she tried to control her breaths, they came fast and shallow.

She looked back at the glass and his face was gone.

Bruce. Bruce was gone.

She swallowed down the lump in her throat. Of course he was gone. A whole damned year and she still couldn't find out why. Her aching, determined heart drove her away from everything she ever knew—the city, the chaos, the damned people sucked into their phones and ipods and blue light screens so much they neglected the actual people around them—and her right into Soura Heights. Where life was supposed to be cozy. Where time was supposed to slow down. Where the weather was perpetually sunny and people used their faces to smile instead of emojis on their screens. But that was not what this place was, was it? It was where Bruce was taken away from her. It was where his soul was consumed and his body spat back

14

out for her to bury.

Damn it. I still don't know what did that to him!

No matter how many corners she poked her nose in, there were no solid answers. No one ever knew who Bruce Anderson was. No one knew his charming demeanor. No one remembered his silky voice. According to everyone, Bruce Anderson was just an unfortunate incident they only knew through a passing mention about the forest. Covista Forest—the only corner of Soura Heights her nose hadn't poked into yet.

The gold embroidered man on the polo shirt taunted her, begging her to stand up, stand up and look.

"What for? Huh? That clean, crisp white shirt? You think that's worth looking at?" Fey was unable to control herself, lashing out at a mannequin behind the glass.

A sour taste crept in the back of her mouth and she clenched her jaws to keep it down.

I'm not throwing up. Not now.

As her heartbeat radiated in her ears, she held them closed with her fists.

"Stop it!" she yelled out to no one in particular, and shut her eyes tight. Red splotches spattered against the inside of her eyelids and she screamed out loud again to stop them from multiplying. She was afraid if she kept them open, her dizziness would make her pass out.

The glass vibrated under her hand when she threw her fist against it.

"Not now! This isn't happening now!"

Fey, you have got to stop.

Collapsing to the ground, she tried to keep herself from crying, from letting all the pent up emotions spill out. Anger, confusion, anxiousness. She let out another wail when grief struck her.

Come on, Fey. Get it together!

Just then, she felt someone's presence behind her. It hovered over her like a shadow. Fey swallowed hard. This wasn't the time for small town pleasantries.

15

A wrinkled hand touched her shoulder and Fey realized Louise Schniber, Soura Heights's resident town crazy, was standing behind her.

What now? Fey was annoyed. As if she wasn't already struggling enough, she had to deal with Louise and her ramblings.

"The Earth calls to the walls and stops them from shaking."

Fey unwrapped her fists and felt the cobblestone underneath her. Cold. Smooth. Her breaths deepened and the vise loosened from around her chest. She opened her eyes and realized the dizzying feeling had faded.

Thank God. It's passing.

Fey stood up and faced Louise. The old woman's eyes were their typical wide saucers.

"Hi, Louise," Fey managed out. Louise's breath smelled sour when she leaned inches away from Fey.

"Rising for intent. It's the lynx's purpose. Her kitty cat whiskers must sense that, too."

Louise's nonsense was nothing new. She spent her days wandering the streets, spouting off in riddles. She spent her nights alone at home, a few doors down from Fey.

"Sure, Louise. Listen. I'm feeling a little tired. I think I'm going to go visit Frankie. Need me to pick you up a slice?"

Louise's eyes bulged out even further. She clasped her hands together over her mouth and violently shook her head. She silently backed up, almost tripping over her tattered skirt. She turned and ran, disappearing from the cobblestone road.

Fey turned back around to face the display window. That stupid shirt was still there, still mocking her and her ignorance. A bitter taste was left in the back of her throat.

Damn it.

"I'll never understand how you can eat that."

With a look of disgust, Frankie slid Fey a slice of apple pie with cheddar melted on top. Behind her sat shelves piled high with artisan pies. Each one was baked fresh for the day and served out to the small-town community. The top shelf was reserved for the only revolving flavor. It was always some result of an experimental taste test.

"Maybe you should try it sometime." Fey sleepily smiled back at her friend with a fork full of sticky pie. It tasted exactly as she expected; a sweet and salty flood of memories. A single bite and a wave of the past washed over her, stinging her eyes.

"You're thinkin' of Bruce again, aren't you?" Frankie gave a heavy sigh as she fished a towel from her apron pocket and wiped down the booth across from Fey. She sat, facing Fey with legs crossed and an elbow on the table. "You know how you get when you think of him, now."

"I know," Fey said. "I can't help it. It's been almost a full year. 361 days." She took another bite off her fork and winced at the reaction on her senses. "You know, I never had cheese on pie until he insisted I try it. He said it was a tradition from France, but really it originated in England, but with a completely different cheese. I never did correct him on it. We just called it celebration pie anyway."

"I'm surprised you didn't correct him." Frankie rolled her eyes. A red curl dropped in front of her face. "Sometimes, you're too smart for your own good." She grabbed the plate from Fey's reach. "Some celebration that is. It has you goin' all weepy eyed on me."

"Hey!"

"Hey nothin'. You hang tight, got it?"

Frankie swiveled her knees outside the bench and carried the plate to the kitchen. Fey watched as her best friend of nearly a year disappeared behind the swinging doors. She took a sip of her tea.

Ugh. I wish Frankie would invest in coffee beans.

Frankie's teas were always some sort of earthy blend. They looked pretty in the glass display jars, like colorful potpourri, but it never tasted right to Fey. It was like drinking flower petals.

Frankie reappeared seconds later with an empty plate in her hand. She filled it with a slice from the top shelf of the pie tower. The label above it read: **Pie of the Week**. She brought the plate back over and slid it over to Fey's seat.

"Here. Try this instead."

Fey picked up her fork and poked the crust. "What's this?" She knew it could be anything from a frozen raspberry lemonade to a gummy bear and saffron strudel.

"Vinegar pie!" Frankie threw her hand in the air with a flourish, making her red curls bounce by her ears. "It's this week's specialty." She cupped her hand to the side of her mouth and whispered, "The secret is a pinch of picklin' salt."

"And you think cheese on pie is peculiar?"

Frankie smiled at her, revealing a dimple in her left cheek. "Peculiar? No, Fey, it's just weird. Eat up. It'll make you forget all about your sadness." Frankie watched her poke at the slice with her fork for a few seconds before she remembered something else. "Oh! I nearly forgot!" She reached into her apron pocket and pulled out a tiny brown bag. She unrolled the top and dipped her fingers in. She pulled out a few crystals and placed them on top of Fey's slice. "Sugar crystals! Claire threw them in for me in the last order I made. Don't they just dress it up nicely? Pretty it up a little?"

Fey nodded, though she wondered if her teeth would bite through them.

"And I bet you're already feeling better with a pretty little pie in front of you."

Fey nodded again. She pinched one of the crystals with her fingers and placed it in her mouth.

They're like rocks.

Frankie reached out and fingered a section of Fey's hair. "You know what else might make you feel a bit better? Your hair could use a good trim."

Fey pulled her hair out of Frankie's fingers. Sure, it was a little longer than she normally had it, but she liked the blunt cut. She thought it suited her. A plain-Jane haircut for plain-Jane Fey.

Frankie brushed her own hair out of her eyes, "Oh! I heard about your… episode today. You are so strong, you know?"

"Episode?"

Small town talk spreads too damned quickly.

"It was nothing, Frankie. I just felt voracious. Needed to get something in my stomach."

"Ha! You mean you were hungry. Sure, I get that. Still though, yelling out like that in the streets and then brushing it off like nothing? You are strong."

Strong has nothing to do with it.

Regardless if she felt it or not, Fey liked Frankie complimenting her on strength. It made her feel like she was able to stand on her own feet without needing support from anyone. Frankie had been calling her strong since the day Fey moved to Soura Heights. It was what made her feel an instant connection, like she had found the Anne to her Diana.

"Hey!" a deep voice interrupted from a couple tables over. "I know you're not giving away my slice to someone else, Frankie!"

Without looking over her shoulder, Frankie replied, "Oh, you hang on to those horses of yours, Tom. I'll get to you in a minute."

She gave Fey a wink. "Guess I better take care of the sheriff's order. He can't go back to duty on an empty stomach, you know." She grabbed a spare fork from her apron pocket and swiped a bite from Fey's plate. "Hm. Next time, I'll use more nutmeg. You really should try it, though. It's like apple pie, but better. It'll snatch those tears out of your eyes and make you think of better things. Like that birthday of yours we need to plan. It's only four days away!" She threw Fey a second wink as she leapt up from the table.

Frankie ran over to Tom, where he waited with his fingers drumming the table. Tom's wife, Peggy, sat in front of him and from across the room, Fey could see her smile at Frankie, clearly apologizing on his behalf for his outburst.

Frankie really had a way with people. Every day, she buzzed from table to table handing out knowing winks and comforting nudges. She asked about their love lives, gave advice to every conundrum, and reminded them when their hair grew enough for a haircut. She was a cornerstone for their small town who everyone knew well and loved often. Without Frankie, it was likely all of Soura Heights would become unglued.

Fey gobbled up the rest of her pie, wincing at the bitter taste. She dug out some cash from her jeans pocket and left it on the table. In the opposite corner, Frankie was chatting with a man she didn't recognize, a hard feat in a town where everyone knew everyone.

Weird. No one just passes through Soura unless they have a reason.

She watched as Frankie took a menu from him, her hand flipping through the air. Frankie's expression shifted from comforting ease to a stoic control. It was the same expression Fey remembered Frankie wearing when she first met her. At a time when she was losing control over her own life, it had felt good to have someone else claim the control for her. Now, she watched Frankie address this man in the same way. If this stranger was looking for an escape from his day-to-day, then he came to the right place—right in Frankie's hands where she could guide him away from his chaos and right into her method of satisfaction.

His face, seemingly well to do and a clean cut city boy, appeared out of place. No doubt Frankie was charming him with her dimples and small town witticisms. He adjusted the top button of his plaid shirt. Even his clothes stuck out. None of the men in Soura wore cuffed sleeves or silver buttons. Their plaids were lumberjack fleece. If they had felt fancy, maybe they'd wear a polo shirt.

That damned polo shirt.

Fey felt heat rising in her again. She cooled it off with another swig of tea.

From the out-of-town man's table, Frankie looked up at Fey. Even through her chatter, she took the time to wave goodbye. "See ya, Buttercup!"

Buttercup. Fey rolled her eyes at the nickname Frankie gave her a month into her move to Soura Heights.

"Here's your tea!" Frankie placed a hot cup in front of her. She wrinkled her nose at the smell; a mixture of flowers and citrus.

"Do you have any coffee?"

Frankie flipped her hand in the air and scoffed. "Coffee? Absolutely not! Have you seen the display in front?" She pointed at the counter. "I create each blend with these hands myself. You're not gonna find tea like this

20

anywhere else, trust me on that!"

Fey lifted the cup to sip from the liquid inside. The hot drink hit her lips. It tasted exactly like it smelled. Like liquid garden weeds.

"Ain't it good?" Frankie leaned on the table, urging her for praise.

Fey nodded. If coffee wasn't an option, then this was what she would choke down. She took another sip and noticed something loop from the bottom of the cup and float to the surface. Using her spoon, she scooped it out and examined it. It looked like a small yellow petal. It reminded her of the patch of buttercups that used to grow in front of her apartment in Saint Paign.

"Buttercups?"

It was Frankie's turn to crinkle her nose. "What did you say?"

Fey held up the yellow petal in question. "Buttercups. Did you put buttercups in your tea?"

Frankie threw her head back and cackled to the ceiling. "Buttercups? Ha! That's a laugh! No, you've got a bit of dandelion there. Don't you taste it? Dandelion and lime." She laughed again, obnoxiously loud.

How the hell was Fey supposed to know what dandelions tasted like?

"Hey, that's what I'm gonna call you. Sound good, Buttercup?"

Fey waved goodbye again to Frankie.

"Don't forget to pay a visit to Claire for me!" Frankie called over her shoulder.

Fey heard the bells on the door tinkle behind her as she left Pie-Pie For Now. Every shop on Busy Street had a signature chime, unique to their own. Fey would have thought this was part of the small town charm she always wanted. But some days, it felt more pretentious than the city life she had left behind.

A little over a year ago, and I would have begged for

anomalous bells.

She blinked in the light on Busy Street. Claire's herb shop, You Herb It Here First, was just a few doors down. Fey took it upon herself to pick up orders for Frankie, but that meant today she would have to pass the same window she passed before. Feeling the bitter pie in her stomach, she wanted to avoid that display.

She could only imagine what kind of wild rumors would fly around town with two public panic attacks in one day.

CHAPTER TWO

One Year + Six Months Earlier

Fey interlocked her fingers into Bruce's. Their palms touched and Fey's heart leapt as everything felt right in place.

Bang. Bang. Bang.

Well, everything except the people in the apartment above them. Every time their feet hit the floor, it shook the ceiling.

She blinked her eyes at Bruce. If she had to endure thin walls and loud neighbors, she would, so long as this was the face she would wake up to every morning.

They were six months into their newlywed bliss, but neither set of parents approved.

"You're too young," her mother told her.

Her father's argument was always, "He can't afford to take care of you."

Bruce's parents were quiet all through the wedding, but their silent crossed arms had said enough. None of that mattered to either Bruce or Fey. It didn't matter that they were right out of high school. Their hearts beat for each other and that was all that mattered.

Fey was born and raised in the city of Saint Paign. Even though it wasn't as large as New York or Los Angeles, she felt lost in it just the same. It was loud and crowded, even through the high school halls.

Often, she found herself receding into herself between classes, avoiding the eventual bump into one of the girls who'd laugh at her lackluster clothes or lack of makeup. No one was more surprised than Fey when she found Bruce waiting for her after class and walking down the wrong hall just to pass her locker.

To her, Bruce was an out-of-reach baseball player with the ability to charm the dimples off Eliza Dushku. He drifted from clique to clique, chatting up everyone from the burnouts to the brains. But, since she was a singleton without an entourage full of people who were clones of herself, she didn't have the pleasure of fitting in enough to earn herself a conversation with Bruce Anderson.

That was until they were paired up in a home economics class.

"And the last pair for today's lesson is Bruce and Fey. Okay everyone, grab your aprons."

Fey blushed as her hand brushed up against Bruce's. They had reached for the same apron hook.

"Oh sorry, you can have the one with the toad on it." *Bruce pulled it off the hook and slipped it over her head. He pointed to the picture on the front and read the pun, "Toaday's the Day!"*

"It's a frog, actually." *Fey had no idea what she was doing, correcting the boy everyone else fawned over.*

"Is that so? How'd you know that?"

"Its skin is smooth and green. Frogs use a coating of mucus to breathe through their skin. Toads have dry, bumpy skin." *She bit the inside of her cheek to stop herself from continuing.*

But Bruce looked at her with inquisitive eyes and gave her a smile. She had never noticed from afar, but he had a little crooked tooth at the bottom. She liked that.

Her bite didn't work. "Most frogs have teeth on their upper jaw so they can pin down prey before they swallow it. Toads don't have any."

Bruce grabbed a second apron. This one had a simple drawing of a spatula on the front. As he wrapped the ties around his waist, he continued listening.

"There's actually a type of frog called a glass frog that has clear skin. You can watch its lungs move as it breathes. And another that doesn't even have lungs at all. It only uses its skin."

Fey felt herself flush and wished she could stop herself from talking.

She shrugged her shoulders. "I read a lot."

He exhaled slowly and nodded. "I like that."

"All right class! Today, we're going to learn how to bake chocolate pie. It's the easiest recipe there is and I already have the dough ready for you."

Now, in their own apartment, Fey could claim Bruce to herself. There was no competition from girls who were prettier or better with their words.

She ran her fingers through his hair and squeezed him close. "Bruce?"

"Yeah?"

"Do you think I'll ever use that oven in there?" Fey pointed to the tiny kitchen behind the dining room. Her heartbeat rose from just thinking about turning the knobs on. She looked back at him and swallowed hard. Heat ran to her ears, afraid of how he might answer. If he expected her to cook their meals with anything but the microwave, she would have a hard time tearing herself away from the fetal position on the ground. There was no way she could do it. Not without dealing with the hard set notion of panic.

He squinted his eyes in the direction and shrugged his shoulders. "I don't know, Honey Pot. But you don't have to. You never have to. I can always bring home something from the store. You know, they let us have first pick at the end of our shift of whatever they're going to throw out. We can live off that for a while and you won't have to touch any of those knobs."

The heat drained from her ears and she exhaled with relief. "Yeah, I supposed we could."

She wished she could get over it. She wished she knew how to move on and act like the adult she was supposed to be. She moved her hand to her left wrist. The scar had barely faded, but the memory was still fresh.

"Everyone out! Out of the classroom! Now!" The home economics teacher was screaming for the class to evacuate the classroom in a panic. She was running in circles, corralling teenagers who were frozen to the spot with gaping mouths.

25

But Fey couldn't move. She was on the ground, holding her arm, holding her tears at bay.

It had all happened so fast. The teacher instructed the class to check on their projects to see their progress. Bruce had stood back, gesturing to the oven door for Fey to do the honors.

Nervous, she had opened it a little too fast. She didn't have time to notice the pie had spilled out. It wasn't until the flames hit her arm that she realized something had gone wrong.

Before she knew it, she was rolling on the floor to put out the flames on her apron and arm. The flames licked her skin clean. She hugged her wrist tight to her chest, and prayed this was a dream. From her position on the floor, she felt like a bird with a damaged wing, with a room full of spectators wondering how to step over her without dirtying their shoes.

"I said everyone out! You!" The teacher touched Bruce by the shoulder. "Go get someone from the office for help!"

But Bruce shook his head. "No, ma'am. She's my partner. I'm not leaving her alone."

As a red-headed girl ran out of the room to get help, Bruce knelt down beside Fey. Her eyes were watery, but she didn't need to choke back her tears anymore. Bruce's hand on her forehead stopped them for her.

"Besides frogs, what else do you read about?"

CHAPTER THREE

Present Day

Somehow, Fey made it to You Herb It Here First without falling into the display trap. She pushed the image of that stupid mannequin in the back of her mind and blocked her it from her sight when she passed the window. She sighed in relief when she walked through the shop doors, a bell like a baritone's giggle welcoming her.

"Hey, Claire."

Claire's blonde bob swung behind her ears as she looked up from the magazine she was thumbing through. "Fey! Good to see you. I'm assuming you're here to pick up the next order?" Her voice was always cheerful even though her eyes were often tired.

"Yup. Frankie asked if I could pick it up while I was out."

"Let's see..." Claire crouched down below the cashier's counter. She shifted a few bags around and pulled out a doll with ratty yarn hair. She shook her head. "Oh BettyAnne. She's been looking for her doll for days." BettyAnne was Claire's daughter. She was one of the town's only residents under the age of ten. For a five-year-old, she was pretty well in tune to people's emotions. Fey always felt nervous around her; not because she didn't know how to be around kids, but because she didn't know how to be around people with that much empathy. "Here we are!" Claire lifted a large paper bag and placed it on the counter top. "Be careful, now. It's heavy. There are three kinds of sugar in there."

"Thanks, Claire. I'll make sure she gets--"

"Oh wait! There's one more thing!" Claire ran to a shelf and quickly scooped something dry and crumbly into a clear plastic bag. She zipped it up and handed it to Fey. "Valerian root. Smells like feet, but it can do amazing things in small doses to the right recipe. Frankie asked me to add it to her order when it came in. Here you go."

"Thanks, Claire."

Fey took the bag in her hand and lightly shook it. The

27

substance inside was like crumbled moss. Something about the way it sat inside the bag was unsettling. Even though it was dried and dead, Fey felt it looked like the same wet plants that attached themselves to rocks, creating slimy surfaces that rubbed off on your skin when you touched it.

Next week's specialty pie is going to be interesting.

She elbowed the door, signaling the baritone chimes again as she left. To the left was Frankie's pie shop, a few doors down. To the right, Rosewood Court. Fey decided to turn right to tote the bag back home. There was no need to risk being fed a second slice of vinegar pie in a single day, nor another run-in with the shop window.

On her walk home, Fey passed the pun-named shops, wondering who made that executive decision.

Executive. Not a word that belongs in Soura.

Someone must have thought there should be a drop of humor in a pool of meek women and meeker men. But just like the individual bell chimes in every shop, Fey abhorred the idea. The charm was lost on her. It was like the town was covering up something dark with tasteless humor. The only pun she could stomach was the bookstore: A Pair of Dice Lost. Not because she thought it was funny. It wasn't. But she found humor when the literary reference went over the heads of ill-read residents.

The used bookstore was at the end of Busy Street, right where Fey turned to make her way toward Rosewood. It was one of the first places she stepped foot in after her move to Soura Heights. To this day, it was one of the places she truly felt welcome.

"Hello?"

The air in the bookstore smelled of a musty sweetness. Her heart fluttered. The faded scent of ink told Fey that this was her favorite kind of bookstore; used. She looked around at the vast shelves. Each cover had been held and loved by others. Each page corner had been flipped by someone else's hands. There was a story behind each book's ownership that was just as strong as the one within its pages. Yes, there would be something useful here.

Fey breathed in the air again. It held a hint of faint chocolate, drawing her in further. "Hello?"

A squeak came from behind the front counter. Fey hadn't noticed the rocking chair at first. The woman who sat in it was quiet as a mouse and peeped over a book in her lap with a nod.

"Oh, hi. I um..." Fey wasn't sure exactly what she was looking for. "I was wondering if you could help me find a book."

The woman hitched a graying eyebrow.

"I need a book on..." Fey thought carefully about what to ask for. "I need a medical book."

The rocking chair woman huffed and Fey realized she must have sounded crazy. She felt crazy. "You know, something to have on hand at home. Something that could be...useful in case..." She thought quickly. "In case I burn myself on the stove or, you know, hit my head or something." That sounded normal, right?

With another huff, the rocking chair woman pointed to a shelf in the far right corner. After a few minutes of shelf-surfing, Fey found something. The cover held a portrait silhouette and a stethoscope weaving around its neck. Inside the black silhouette was a crude outline of a brain: **Guidance on Traumatic Brain Injury.**

Fey made her own huffing noise. This wasn't her normal read. She wasn't looking forward to flipping through its pages. But she hoped it held the information she was determined to find.

She noticed a man, the same man she saw chatting with Frankie at the pie shop. The same man in the plaid shirt with silver buttons.

Who the hell is that?

He was leaning against the bookstore, cell phone in hand, thumb scrolling meaninglessly. Fey rolled her eyes. Her own cell phone was left at home, uncharged. She always felt like they

29

prevented making real connections.

Stupid phones.

She had thought about approaching him, but before she could, a voice on the opposite side of the street distracted her.

"They'll be singing before you know it! All their songs come again and again. They're old records that can't be shattered!" Louise Schniber was yelling across the street.

Ignoring Louise, Fey turned back around to the plaid shirt man, but he was gone. Fey shrugged off the feeling of uncertainty and continued her way home.

"Hi Fern!" Fey called out to her potted plant when she walked in the front door. She ran her hand along the bookcase against the wall. "And hello to you, too, friends."

Her ranch style home allowed her to relax. Filled with the thrift store furniture she and Bruce hastily bought for their apartment, it felt comforting. She stretched her neck backward and looked toward the ceiling. Unlike the apartment she left behind, she was able to move freely within her space. No feet patrolling the ceiling, no cars parading a parking lot. Just her, her books, and Fern.

How she wished she could share this space with Bruce. He would have loved to set up the spare bedroom as a hobby space full of gadgets to tinker with. She would have been happy for him to take their own television in there, too. Maybe they could have added a shelf to store his DVD collection. It would have been his place to feel comfortable; to shut the door and tinker while she curled into the big living room chair with a book in one hand and coffee in the other. Instead, the room that would have been Bruce's sat unoccupied, storing boxes of things she didn't know where to place behind a closed door she rarely opened. When she moved here a year ago, she didn't know what to do with space that didn't exist in the apartment.

She placed the brown bag on top of the island counter. She took another look at the valerian root, shrugged her shoulders, and placed it inside the bag with everything else. She assured herself whatever was in there could wait for tomorrow. After all, as Frankie said, there was a party to plan.

A party. What an inscrutable thing to plan when you're 20.

Fey sat in her oversized chair by the window, her faithful bookcase within arm's reach. She bit her lip, looking at the second shelf. There, her medical book, her *traumatic brain injury* book sat useless. She had read the most important pages so many times, she had them memorized. But she still didn't have the answers she was looking for. She feared her answers weren't going to be found within a book. No, she needed to do more.

She breathed out her disdain and turned to face the window instead, where she could see the sequoia and sycamore treetops of Covista Forest. Somewhere beyond her view, the trees parted to reveal a main trail. Though she hadn't dared to step foot into those woods herself, she knew it was there. She also knew there was a place off the trail. A place where people stepped off and were somehow swallowed whole.

"The forest just eats them up." That was what Sheriff Brickshaw had told her.

How the hell does that happen?

The trees' tips jutted out like pointed teeth in the distance. Every time she looked out the window, a voice told her to steer clear.

Stay out of the forest.

The taste of sour memories crept up in the back of her throat.

Fey's head spun again. She felt sick to her stomach and again, red splotches splayed against the back of her eyes as she closed them.

Stay out of the forest.

It was what she had heard echo in her thoughts since the day she moved to small-town Soura Heights.

Stay out of the forest.

There was nothing she needed there. She belonged here, in the tiny town safely filled with timid residents.

Stay out of the forest.

It was like a skipping record played over and over every time she looked out of the back window.

But then, the record skipped to another track. Fey forced those words out of her head so she could focus on the new track.

You are a strong woman.

Frankie's words resonated with her as a reminder that she could do anything. But was she strong *enough*?

Getting up from her seat, she made her way to the hanging planter in the kitchen. Fern's soil was dry, so she gave the thirsty plant a drink from the watering can. When the plant first came home, she didn't know if she'd be able to keep it alive. It felt weird, like it had been watching her, waiting for an opening to overgrow and take over. But as time passed, she felt comfort in caring for it. She watched the leafy fronds perk up almost instantly, almost thankfully. Fern hadn't been so scary after all. If she could handle one fear, surely she could handle more.

And just like that, she knew what she wanted to do to celebrate her 21st birthday in a few days. She was going to face the forest. She was going to face where Bruce was taken from her. She was going to give herself the closure she had been denied all this time.

CHAPTER FOUR

One Year + Five Months Earlier

Fey sat with a loose pile of papers on her lap. She had collected them from coffee shop community boards in Saint Paign, hoping to find available work. She had spent most of her day being shuffled through the foot traffic, in search of paper flyers. She hated how crowded it felt when she was out, but not as much as the shame of sifting through online listings. She picked one up: **Be your own boss and look great, too!** There was a picture of a woman drinking a shake in a bathing suit.

So far, no luck.

She glanced at the computer in front of her and felt herself flush. Even the thought of charging it up made her sweat.

Damn technology.

She popped a new piece of gum in her mouth. The old one had lost its flavor. She always felt like the more time people stuck their faces into screens, the more time they took away from developing connections with real people. Technology was great... until connections were only digital.

Bruce had encouraged her to search online. "It would be easier, faster," he said. She hated that he was right.

As she contemplated the piled papers on her lap, she heard the front door. Bruce was home from work, with a hanging planter swinging from his fingers. It wasn't unusual for him to come home from Nonni's with day-old groceries, but a plant?

The hell is this?

Curious, Fey stood up from her perch and followed him into their tiny kitchen where he hung it on a hook by the window. He turned around and spread his arm out, presenting the new occupant to her. "A fern!"

Fey's eyes grew wide.

A fern?

Fey's thumb never favored the color green. She could never figure out what plants wanted from her. If it were true that plants needed only soil, sun, and water, then the few times she had tried potted plants, it wouldn't have ended the way it did. The lilies she had years ago turned brown before they ever bloomed. The leaves on a violet shriveled the day after she brought the plant home. Once, she even tried to care for a potted cactus, but the thorns fell out and the soil rejected what was left. Fey was convinced plants would rather choose death than her.

The only experience Fey ever had with a fern was out of a favorite childhood story. Most people would remember the final scene where Billy finds a red fern growing from his dogs' graves. Fey, however, always pictured a different scene entirely: Billy by the giant sycamore tree in the forest, his dogs chasing away the threat of a mountain lion.

Fey's horticultural training didn't prepare her thumb to take care of a plant that should be living in a place full of sycamores, wildcats, and God knows what else.

"A fern?"

"Yeah! The florist at work got a new shipment in and let us take home any of the old plants we wanted. Some were a little sadder than others, but this fern seemed to be doing pretty well. Doesn't it make it feel more like… a home? You know, to have something here to take care of? Something to liven up the place a bit?"

Fey shrugged her shoulders. "Sure." Her eyes narrowed as she looked over the crevices on the leaves and the hanging pot it sat in. She imagined a family of ferns scattered along the forest floor at the base of a large sycamore tree. It made the hair on her neck stand on end.

Bruce must have noticed her noticing it. "What's up, Fey? Something wrong?"

"Wrong? No. Nothing's wrong. It just got me thinking."

God, I can't have this thing in my home.

Bruce slid his arms around her waist and brought her close to him. "What's it got you thinking about, Honey Pot?" He instinctively knew when Fey's nerves spiked and knew how to diffuse them. His ridiculous pet name got to her every time.

Bruce's hands drummed on the table in front of her. Fey had never been to a restaurant with a boy before, especially one as nice as Streetwise Tavern. But here she was, on a date with the boy she and every other 16-year-old girl dreamt of.

She opened the menu and was shocked to see there were no prices under any of the entrees. She supposed this was the reason her parents let her out. If he could afford to pay blindly for a meal, then he would be all right in their books.

Fey couldn't tell if he was twitching from first-date jitters or if the menu made him nervous, too.

"Hello. My name is Gregorio, and I will be your server this evening. Can I interest you in today's special? We have a grilled mahi mahi with artichoke caponata. It comes in a sweetened white wine vinegar sauce and a side of roasted acorn squash wedges."

Fey's eyes must have read as shocked. From across the table, Bruce shared the same expression. The special sounded expensive.

"Um. Can I have a coffee, please? And..." Fey quickly scanned the menu for something that sounded familiarly inexpensive. "A house salad?"

Bruce's expression melted into relief. "The same, please."

When the waiter returned with two coffees, he set down a tray with two porcelain creamers, sugar, and a pot of honey with a honey wand.

Again, Bruce's eyes widened. He pointed to the display on the tray and blurted out, "Honey pot!" The second the words escaped from his mouth, he hid his face in his hands.

"I'm sorry, Fey." He peeked through his fingers and spoke in a low tone. "I don't know what I'm doing here." His

mouth curled up in a nervous smile. "I'm not used to all of this fancy stuff. I just wanted to take you somewhere nice. Somewhere you'd appreciate."

Fey shrugged her shoulders and quietly smiled back at him. She didn't know what to say, but she liked the way he looked at her and she appreciated his effort.

"Honey pot," she echoed. "Yeah, I like that."

"Really? Is that what I should call you?"

It was Fey's turn to blush. "I mean, I think I'd like that in my coffee." She reached for the honey wand and dripped some into her drink.

"Oh, well. I think I might, too."

Bruce did the same and took a drink. He winced. "I don't know why I ordered coffee. I don't even like it. You're right, though. Honey Pot saved the day."

She took another drink of hers.

"I mean, you and the honey pot. You saved it. By suggesting it. I mean. The honey pot. Gosh, what am I saying?"

Fey sipped again. She was afraid if she pulled the drink from her mouth, she would blurt out a list of random facts she memorized from a book she couldn't remember.

"Fey... say something. I'm going a little crazy over here."

"The average bee hive can make up to 200 pounds of honey a year."

Bruce shook his head and coyly smiled. "That brain of yours."

She shook the memory clear as the fern glared at her from the window.

"Nothing special, really. Just reminds me of a book, that's all."

Fey could feel Bruce breathe in the scent of her hair. "Oh, is that so? Which one might that be? *The Borrowers*? *Charlotte's Web*? *Mathilda*? Or the one about the rats of NIMH?"

"Where the Red Fern Grows."

Bruce brushed Fey's hair off her neck and kissed her skin. It tickled and made the hair on her neck stand up again. "I should have guessed. It was staring at me in the title and all." He flipped one of the fern leaves through his fingers. "Except, this one isn't red, so I guess it's not quite the same, huh?" He hugged her closer and rocked her body in a soft sway.

Fey turned around to face Bruce, his arms still wrapped around her waist. She pushed her gum to her cheek pocket to hide it from him. He gave her a playful grin and she could see one slightly crooked bottom tooth. No one ever noticed it except Fey. She always thought of it as a special smile just for her and no one else.

Fey gave Bruce a quick kiss on the lips and slithered out from under his arm, leaving him in want of more physical attention. She led him over to a shelf full of childhood novels. She instantly found the blue spine she was looking for.

She flipped the pages straight to Chapter 19. Skimming the first few paragraphs jolted her right back in the story she remembered. She thrust the book over to Bruce, pointing to the open pages. "Here, see?" She moved her gum to the other cheek.

Bruce took it in his hands to appease her. "Billy...coons...Ol Dan...mountain lion? Honey Pot, you're going to have to break it down for me." He handed the book back to her.

Fey sighed. "Billy's in the forest, hunting with his dogs. They had to chase away a precocious mountain lion. Only, one of his dogs expires soon after."

"Precocious, huh?" Bruce smiled. It was *her* smile. "You mean it was dangerous?"

Fey ran her hand across the pages gingerly. She felt as if she were right there with Billy, hearing Dan cry out in both bravery and pain. She could feel the forest earth under her and smell the open-air scent. She felt her palms sweat with fear, knowing how the final pages read. She looked up at Bruce. "You must think I'm crazy."

Bruce carefully took the book back, closed the covers, and placed it back home on the shelf. He ran his hand down her arm and brought her body closer to his, placing her arm around his middle. He smoothed the hair on the top of her head and tucked the strays behind her ear.

"Crazy? No. Crazy isn't a thing. It's a silly concept that isn't even real. That head of yours, though, it's something else, isn't it? Being able to recall a specific place in a book and find it in an instant. I still don't see how you got all that from a plant. Fey, you aren't crazy. You are something else entirely." He lifted her chin up, kissed her once, then stopped. "But first, this." He tapped her lips.

Instinctively, she moved her gum from her cheek and presented it to him between her teeth. With two fingers, he plucked it from its place, freeing her mouth for a kiss.

Kissing Bruce never failed to turn her knees weak. Returning the favor, she lifted herself on her toes, supporting herself from collapsing as much as possible. She knew within minutes, his hands would find their way to the clasps of her undergarments and he would lead her back to their bedroom where they would find their familiar physical tempos and she would welcome his body into hers.

Fey lay against Bruce's chest, feeling it rise and fall. She traced the swirly pattern in his chest hair with her fingers and felt his fingers mimic the same pattern on her back. Being right here, in this position and within their bedroom walls, felt safe. They were safely tucked in away from the danger of the forest.

Fey could feel Bruce adjust his weight slightly. "I bet you're still thinking about those books of yours, huh?" he asked. "Not even I can shake them from you."

Fey felt Bruce's arms hug her tight before he let go to dress. As she heard his pants zip, she called out to him, "Going to go water Fern?"

"Fern? I like that. It's a fitting name, isn't it?" He turned around and winked back at her, then he pulled his shirt over his head and walked out of the room.

Laying in bed, Fey thought of the strange plant Bruce brought home. Here she was, naming something she never planned to dote on. She just hoped it wouldn't choose death over her. She reached for another stick of gum and shivered. A weird thought crept into her mind.

What if it chose death for *me?*

"Keep that gum out of your mouth. It's bad for your teeth!" Bruce called from the kitchen.

She placed it back on the nightstand and gathered her clothes from the floor.

It's just a plant, Fey. The damned thing is harmless, she thought as she joined him in the kitchen.

Bruce pulled back the tiny watering can from the plant. "Still think this thing reminds you of that book of yours?"

She gave him a deadpan look.

Bruce put the watering can down on the counter. "Okay. I'll bite. Tell me about it."

"Didn't I already?"

"Tell me more. I know that brain of yours has more to say. I want to hear it."

Fey shrugged. "You know how you get absorbed into movies?"

Bruce nodded.

"And you know how you make karate-like movements when Chuck Norris is present on screen?" Fey poorly attempted a tiny karate chop in the air. "Like that?"

"I do that?" Bruce's cheeks turned red.

"Every time, and you don't even realize it. It's like that for me every time I get to a good chapter. I'm sucked in. I know where I am—on the couch, in a chair, under a tree—but it feels like I'm present with the character, feeling everything they feel. Fighting everything they fight."

Bruce nodded and karate-chopped right back at Fey. She giggled.

"I read that book for the first time in grade school. I remember being on the playground. I remember hearing the kids all around me. But I also remember it didn't feel like the playground at all. I was right there with Billy. I *was* Billy. I was there, in the woods feeling panicked and apprehensive. I felt the tree bark on my back. I saw ferns blanketing the ground. I smelt the wild animal's breath when it shouted its cry. I felt the deceased dog's fur, matted with blood and dirt. I was in the forest, with Billy and the dogs and all the ferns, just like this one."

Bruce wrapped an arm around her. "The forest, huh? That's what this reminds you of?" He jerked his head to the side, using his temple to point to Fern.

Fey quietly nodded.

"Well, then." He brushed her hair behind her ears. "Who knows where Fern came from. Probably a delivery truck." He gestured around their tiny apartment. "I can tell you this, though: there isn't a forest anywhere like that around here. There are no mountain lions. No massive amount of trees. No dying dogs. Just a single fern. Fern. That's it. My suggestion? If you ever come across a forest like that, stay out of it." Bruce brushed the side of her cheek. His voice was low and protective. "Stay out of the forest. Stay here with me, instead."

"Stay out of the forest?"

"Stay out of the forest."

And there it was, *her* smile again.

CHAPTER FIVE

Present Day

Fey slipped a worn, dusty book off the shelf. She was in the bookstore as often as she was home. The books on the shelves called to her like old friends, begging to tell her their stories again or for the first time, it didn't matter. Sometimes, the books themselves were home.

Fey heard a sniffle behind her. Miss Davis was at her perch in an old chair by the front. No one knew her first name. Everyone only knew her as Miss Davis, and she saw to it that no one knew much else about her. She was a quiet store owner who was short of words. Fey thought about how quickly word spread about her 'episode'.

Probably the only way she's survived so long here.

"Hey, Miss Davis," Fey called out to her.

Miss Davis ran her hand under her nose in response.

"Um, do you have any botany books in stock?"

Miss Davis threw her finger in the air. It wagged to the right.

"Thank you."

Fey followed the direction Miss Davis had directed her. The inventory system was chaos. Nothing was labeled, books weren't organized by author name or even by genre. But Miss Davis still knew where every novel lived. Her finger searched out any title you asked for like a dowsing rod. Fey's finger scanned the spines and found what she was looking for: a book on caring for indoor plants. Though Fern seemed to be doing well, something told Fey she needed to make sure her only houseplant was protected as much as possible. Miss Davis's magic finger had worked yet again.

Fey pulled the book from its place and walked it over to the register.

If only Bruce could see me now, planning out my afternoon doting on a plant.

She placed the book down on the front counter. "Just this please, Miss Davis."

Miss Davis grunted at her, which was Fey's cue to hand her payment. As Fey waited for a receipt, she ran her fingers through her hair.

"Miss Davis, could I ask your opinion?"

Miss Davis closed her eyes and angled her ear to hear better.

"Do you think I should cut my hair?"

Ugh. Why the hell am I asking this old bat?

Another grunt, and Miss Davis handed Fey her receipt.

The Intensive Hair salon had two customer chairs. They sat mirroring each other in the tiny room. Most days, only one chair was filled at a time, but once in a while, Ally would service one client with her sheers while another would wait under the cover of a plastic dye bonnet. She prided herself as being the only person in Soura with the ability to cut and style hair. She was also known for her knack of prattling. People talked to Ally the same way they talked to Frankie, with one difference. Frankie kept all those secrets to herself. Ally's mouth tended to regurgitate everything she heard.

Ally pulled Fey's hair over the back of the swivel chair. "So what are we doing with you, today?"

"Just a trim."

Ally played with the ends of her hair. "I can see that you need it. You're a bit overdue, actually. You sure you don't want to change it up a little? I could give you a nice chop to frame your face or add some layers for texture?"

Fey shook her head. "No. I just need a trim, Ally. A couple of inches will suffice."

Ally's left eyebrow rose in disbelief. "You sure? There's a lot I could do to this hair of yours. I have some new color I'd love to mix up. It's in the back right now, but I can put together any shade you'd like. You've got such a great skin tone, almost anything would look great on you, even if you wanted to go nuts and go blue." Ally threw her head back and laughed loudly. "Well, maybe not *blue*!"

Fey laughed nervously. She held her houseplant book on her lap, grasping at its cover.

Why did I even come here?

"I'm good, Ally. Just a trim."

Ally shook her head. "One of these days, I'm going to get you to mix it up. There's nothing quite like changing up your hair to make you feel like a whole different person." She pulled out a spray bottle.

Who the hell would want to be a different person?

Fey pulled her hands into her lap nervously.

"Say, what do you have there? I never noticed that about you..." Ally pointed to the elongated scar on her wrist with the end of her comb.

Fey covered it with her other hand. "Just a scar. No big deal."

Every time she looked at her scar, the memory rushed through her like a violent gust of wind. Privately, Fey thought of the scar like a feather. It even healed with a vein-like crease down the middle. But she dared not share that with anyone. She remembered the faces of her classmates. Only Bruce cared enough to look at her in the eyes and give her *her* smile. Everyone else gawked at her misfortune.

Ally rolled her eyes and sectioned Fey's hair into wet ropes. "Okay, Ms. Fey. Let's try a different topic. Writing anything interesting these days?"

Fey frowned. Her writing was her own. She never understood why other people couldn't just let that be.

"Nothing too provocative."

Ally cackled. "Well, I should hope not! You're not *that* kind of girl, are you?"

Damn it. That's not what I mean.

"What have you been up to, Ally?" Fey knew reversing her question would derail Ally into a different topic.

"Oh, you should have seen Claire come in the other day. Somehow, little BettyAnne got a wad of gum stuck in her bangs. Can you believe it? She was on a walk with the babysitter and the wind just carried her chewed up gum out of her mouth and flung it right up there. When she walked in, the poor girl was nearly in tears. Claire tried everything to get it out at home, too. Peanut butter, mayonnaise, ice cubes, and lemon juice. She even tried melting it with a hairdryer, but you can imagine how that worked out." Ally let out another cackle. "Poor girl was nearly covered from eyebrow to chin with everything she could slather in there." She slapped Fey on the shoulder with her comb and laughed loudly again. "She smelled like a kitchen sink!"

Fey thought about BettyAnne walking into the salon with big, watery eyes. No doubt, she would have been upset, worried about adding to her mother's already tired shoulders. Ally's cackling probably didn't help.

Fey let her eyes wander as Ally continued to work. Without moving her neck, she took in the decor. Two tall ceramic vases framed either side of the mirrors. Inside of each was a large bouquet of dried flowers and eucalyptus sprigs. They fanned out to cover a large amount of the wall like deceased 3D wallpaper. Dead plants. It made her stomach churn.

"Hey, you know what I heard the other day? A little birdie came in and told me your birthday is coming up. That's exciting!"

Fey met eyes with Ally through the mirror. "Sure. Later this week."

"Um hm. I hear you're turning 21. I remember being that young. It seems like yesterday, but the amount of grays I have to cover tells me otherwise." Ally paused and pointed the wide tooth comb to her roots. "They multiply overnight. Just a regular gray hair party up here. You're so lucky you don't have to worry about that. Oh well. What do you have planned?"

Fey shrugged her shoulders.

"Um hmm. Well, I hear Ms. Frankie may have something up her sleeves for you. I don't know what exactly, so don't even try to get it out of me." She threw her head back in laughter again. "All I know is that she came in here excited as a six month puppy talking about treating her 'Buttercup' to a day out. Buttercup. Ain't that a cute name for ya?"

Fey rolled her eyes.

That damned nickname.

Suddenly, Ally stopped cutting and put her hand on Fey's shoulder. She leaned in close to whisper, "Did you know that Frankie always asks me to do something with the front of her hair? She just hates that the one curl flops over like a fish in front of her eyes." Ally giggled and slapped Fey's shoulder before resuming her cut.

Fey closed her eyes and pictured Frankie. That little curl was always in front of Frankie's bright blue eyes. But with Frankie's pure confidence, no one would ever know it bothered her. It was a part of her, just one of her inherently charming aspects.

"Why does she hate it?" Fey almost felt bad asking Ally about Frankie's insecurities. It wasn't like her to dive into town gossip. She didn't care to participate in conversation behind anyone's back, especially her best friend. But she also knew Ally was bound to let it out, anyway, so asking was being polite for conversation's sake.

"Oh, Ms. Fey, Frankie never told you? I'm surprised! You two are nearly connected to the hip; best friends like Winnie and Piglet."

Like Anne and Diana.

"Well, I'll tell you, anyway, but don't go telling Ms. Frankie I'm the one blowing her secrets, okay?" Ally chuckled again, clearly enjoying herself. "Apparently, when she was a kid, she fell off the swing in her backyard. She was trying to go as high as she could and - *slip* - she landed butt-first on the ground. When she tried to get up, the swing came flying back at her and just - *bonk* - hit her right in the head. Poor thing got hurt pretty bad. She was knocked out cold. Apparently, she didn't wake up from it until her dad found her a little later and scooped her up. She seemed pretty okay, so he didn't worry too much about it. She just went on being a kid, playing with toys, swinging on swings, wetting the bed, singing without a care in the world." Ally gasped when she paused. "Oh, definitely don't tell her I told you that, okay? Anyway, she told me sometimes she spaced out a little bit. It was like she would fade out of focus here and there. It wasn't until years later they found a blood clot and doctors had to go in and fix it up for her." Ally tapped her comb on Fey's shoulder again. "Imagine that! Poor little Frankie dealing with a blood clot without ever knowing it! Doctors fixed her up and she was good as new, except her hair grew in a little funny where they cut her head open." Ally giggled as she tapped the side of her head. "With a head full of pretty little curls, no one would ever know it unless they asked about that little bit in her face."

45

Ally flipped the comb in her hand to cover her mouth. "Oops. Maybe that was a bit much, huh? Maybe I shouldn't have said anything. Oh well. Shh. We'll keep it a secret between us." She chuckled again and brought the comb back to Fey's hair to pull another section up and over her head. "It shouldn't matter, anyway, since you two are so close. It probably just never occurred to her to say anything to you. You probably have more interesting things to talk about, am I right? More of the things that Poohs and Piglets care about."

Or Annes and Dianas.

Just then, the twinkly chime rang as the salon's door opened. From the corner of her eye, Fey saw a woman with a dark ponytail that swung near her elbows. Her facial expression was lax and she waited by the front desk for Ally to recognize her.

"Oh, June!" Ally's eyes whipped in the mirror to meet the brunette walking in. "I wasn't expecting you. Why don't you have a seat and I'll be with you when I'm all done with Ms. Fey here, okay?" Ally gestured to the only other swivel chair, mirrored right behind Fey. "Are you on break, Ms. June? Or did Frankie give you the day off?"

"I'm on break."

June's voice was as flat as Fey's typical hair. She hardly ever said much, but when she did, people tended to listen. She was blunt, straight to the point, and didn't bother with details that danced around their meaning. Every word June said had a straightforward purpose. Fey could hear the chair behind her squeak as June sat down.

"Ohhh what a fun way to spend your break." Ally's voice sang out at every syllable. "I'm almost done with Ms. Fey over here and then you can tell me what kind of cut you want. I have a few ideas for those long locks of yours." Fey saw her wink in the mirror.

Ally took one last snip at Fey's ends. "And, there you have it, Ms. Fey. Your trim is finished." Her tone sounded unimpressed with the results. "Well, is there anything else I can do for you?"

Fey pulled her hair forward and admired her reflection in the mirror. Despite everything Ally did, her hair still sat squarely above her shoulders. It still looked Plain-Jane as ever, exactly as she was used to, exactly where she was comfortable. She lifted the ends by her fingers and touched the newly clipped strands.

"Thanks, Ally."

"Sure thing, Ms. Fey, sure thing. Maybe later this week, I can convince you to come back in and I'll fix you up a little something for your birthday. After all, a birthday girl has got to have something special, right?"

At the sound of the word birthday, June looked up from her seat. Fey could see June's reflection within her own mirror. It was a reflection of a reflection, a dizzying combination of June's stare and the dead flowers in the vase next to her.

"Your birthday is this week." It wasn't a question. June simply spoke matter-of-factly.

"In three days," Fey responded.

"Hmm." June seemed to be in deep thought. "Plans with Frankie." Again, it wasn't a question. She was speaking in factual pauses.

Ally took a look at both women in her chairs and drummed her comb in the palm of her hand. "Okay, you two Chatty Cathys. Time to cut the small chat up. I've got hair to tackle and I can't do that properly with you two gabbing up the shop!" She threw her head back and laughed as she spun Fey's chair around allowing her to stand up. "Here you are, Ms. Fey. You can leave a payment up front while I handle Ms. June over here. Maybe I can convince her to do something a little fun with *her* locks."

Fey stood out of the chair and walked to the front counter. June continued to stare at Fey from her reflection. It felt like she was watching her, assessing her character from the comfort of her barber chair. It made Fey uneasy.

As Fey opened her wallet with anxious hands, she heard Ally. "All right, Ms. June. What can I do for you today?"

"Whatever you want."

Ally's face lit up. "Oh! Fey! Did you hear that? Someone who knows how to make my day!" Her tone was playfully condescending. "So many options... Really? Whatever I want? Oh wow. Where do I start? We could do a conservative cut a little past your shoulders and add a fringe. Or... Would you be comfortable with a big chop and go pixie?"

As Ally's voice droned into background noise, Fey found enough cash to pay for the cut and tip. She could still feel June's eyes on her, sharp like tacks, even as she walked out the door. The chimes tinkled again and Fey welcomed the fresh air of Busy Street.

From the corner of her eye, she thought she saw a familiar checkered shirt walk by. As she turned for a closer look, her hair whipped in her face, distorting her vision. When she brushed it aside, the checkered pattern was gone. Maybe she hadn't seen him after all. Maybe it was just her imagination.

Fey hugged her book and took a deep breath in. There was an odd earthy scent in the air.

Rain? That's unusual.

She felt in her jeans pocket for a stick of gum, unwrapped one, and popped it in her mouth. If it did rain, she wasn't worried. Rainy days were always mild in Soura. Nothing she couldn't leisurely walk through.

As the wind picked up, she found herself in front of Tell Me Wear. There was the mannequin family, dressed in their same coordinating outfits. She couldn't force herself to stare at the man's shirt like before. She wasn't ready to face another 'episode'. Even still, she could feel a bitter taste rise in her throat and her eyes start to blur.

She tried focusing on the woman mannequin instead, picturing herself in the above-the-knee sundress. She imagined herself in it. In something like that, she would feel exposed, naked, and vulnerable to scrutiny.

Meow.

Was that a cat? She looked around but didn't see one. Maybe she really was imagining things. A gray cloud drifted overhead and light rain fell from the sky. Fey shielded her face with her book and wondered what June meant when she said, "Frankie has plans." Fey didn't want an elaborate celebration. She didn't want balloons or cake or God only knew what Frankie had in store. The only gift she really wanted was the truth of what happened to Bruce.

CHAPTER SIX

It took no time for the sky to open up. Big, fat raindrops fell heavy, coating Fey's fresh haircut and absorbing into her clothes. Her book's pages were soaked through.

So much for Fern.

Lightning cracked through the sky and thunder exploded soon after it. Fey couldn't remember a time when the weather was this relentless. Not here, anyway.

Beep Beep.

Through the downpour, Fey could make out Frankie's golden yellow V.W. bug. Though blurry, it was like a welcoming sunshine through the deluge.

Frankie rolled down the passenger's window. "Get in, ya nut!" she yelled.

Without hesitation, Fey climbed into the passenger's door. Typical. Frankie arrived, ready for her rescue. She felt her clothes soak through the dry seat as she sat down, wincing at the puddle she would no doubt leave behind. "Thanks, Frankie." She almost had to yell over the sound of pounding rain on the windshield.

"No problem. You headin' home?"

"That was my intention." A crack of thunder shot through the sky, making them both jump.

Frankie recomposed herself. "Gotcha. I left the shop in June's hands once she got back from her appointment. You should see what Ally has done to her hair. It's short and shaggy and... I just don't know." She shook her head disapprovingly. "I told her to just trim it, but she didn't listen." Fey could see Frankie's jaw slightly tense up. She thought she saw her eyes darken, too. But then, Frankie blinked and her eyes looked normal again. Fey's own eyes must have been playing tricks on her.

"Anyway, she apparently thinks it's goin' to stop by the time we close, so she can walk home just fine. I guess you didn't get so lucky." Frankie gestured her hand to Fey's wet head.

Fey reached into her jeans pocket and found a few spare napkins. In a vain effort, she wrapped one around a handful of hair and wrung out the water. It soaked up what it could, then tore away and dissolved into gooey blobs in her palm.

Thunder cracked loudly again as another lightning bolt lit up the dark sky.

Keeping her eyes locked on the road, Frankie reached behind her seat and felt around. She brought her hand back to the front and in it was a white hand towel—the same kind used to wipe the tables at Pie-Pie For Now.

"It's a good thing I keep a clean one of these in the car." Frankie tossed the towel into Fey's lap. "This might be a little better than that tiny napkin of yours, Buttercup." Frankie gave her a wink while her eyes focused through the thick rain on the windshield.

Fey nodded a thanks and wrapped her hair in the towel. She squeezed what water she could into it. When she finished, Frankie held her palm out. "Here. I'll take that. You shouldn't keep it on your clothes. They're dirty enough as is." She threw it to the back seat behind her. There, it lay like a drowned, discarded rat.

Next to it sat a cardboard box. Inside was a clay pot with a plant.

That thing has a mouth. No, several mouths.

Fey's palms went sweaty and her mouth dry. "Frankie. What...what is that?"

"What's what?" Frankie glanced in the mirror to see where Fey was pointing. "Oh that? That's a Venus flytrap. I picked him up the other day. I was thinking about gettin' him a friend, too."

Fey looked at its open mouths. Tiny little teeth outlined each one, patiently waiting for a snack. It looked hungry, ready to catch its prey and swallow it whole. Her stomach churned at the thought. "Where... where did you get it?"

"That one? He's actually kind of special. See he's what I call a Covista trap."

"As in... the forest?"

"You got it, Buttercup. There's a bunch of them that grow in there, all along the waterline. If you know where to go, you find plenty of them. June and I found the best spot to find them."

June.

Fey pictured June's cold look the last time she saw her.

"Hey Frankie, how did you and June meet?" The rain was lightening up. The two women no longer had to yell to be heard over it.

Frankie cocked her head to the side, her eyes squinted to focus on the road. "Oh, it wasn't hard, really. She seems like such a loner, doesn't she? But she's just like everyone else. You just have to get her on her own, you know? One-on-one? Actually, she's not much different than you—she's strong, too." She turned down Rosewood Court and another crack of lightning split in the air. "You know, the first day I met her was just like this."

"Rainy?"

"Pourin'. Did you know she lives off of Dover, like me?" Dover Lane was a street down from Rosewood. "She was in her car, but it was hard to see in the nasty rain. There used to be a big pothole at the end of the street. You know, by the big oak on the corner? Everyone knew it was there. We were used to drivin' around it. But it was rainin' so hard that day you couldn't see five feet in front of your windshield. The rain filled in the hole and she hit it. She ended up over correctin' her car and hit that big oak tree on the corner, there. The whole car wrapped around the tree trunk. Poor thing was pretty out of it when I found her."

By now, Frankie had pulled into Fey's driveway and the thunder had subsided to a low rumble. But Fey didn't get up. From the corner of her eye, the Venus flytrap was staring at her, mouths open, silently laughing. She reached for a stick of gum in her pocket to ward off her dry mouth, but it was no use. Whatever was left was soggy and ruined.

"I pulled over and opened her door. She was awake, but groggy. It was like she kept fadin' in and out. I asked if she was okay and she couldn't give me an answer. I don't know if I was thinking clearly, myself. I just knew I had to do somethin'. In the pourin' rain,

I reached inside and pulled her out. Even though we were both soaked through, I got her into my car and drove her back to my place."

Fey furrowed her eyebrows. "You didn't call Tom for help?"

Why is that damned plant staring at me?

Frankie's eyes rolled. "It would have taken Officer Brickshaw ages to get there. And what would he have done? Patted her on the back tellin' her to relax? He might be a kind man, and honest enough, but he's not all too bright. He's just what we have in Soura." Her eyes drifted over to the driver's window and her fingers traced the trails the raindrops left behind. "When I got her home, she was next to nothin', not even awake. She just lay there on the couch, dirty and drenched. But, I cleaned her up. I wiped up the blood and butterflied her forehead shut. I got the leaves out of her hair and put her in a clean set of clothes. She was all fixed up, dressed up as pretty as a pie. It took a good hour, but when June finally woke up, she was back to her normal self, except with a headache. I hate to think about what might have happened to her if I hadn't driven by." Frankie adjusted herself in the seat.

Fey was confused. "She was back to her normal self again? I thought you said this was the first time you met?"

Frankie smiled at her. "Well, I'd seen her around here and there, shoppin' around Busy Street, keepin' her head down, but this was the first time we *really* met. She wasn't an easy one to crack open. But I did. And I found she was strong. She fits right in here, in Soura." Frankie shrugged. "I offered her a job at the pie shop and the rest is history. Once in a while, I need to remind her to smile."

Fey thought back to the times she saw June take over Frankie's shift. She wasn't overly personable. She didn't sit to chat. She didn't offer to brew a tea to pair with a slice of pie. But she was quick about bringing the check and cleaning off tables. She was eagerly efficient, as if she were working for Frankie's approval.

"She's a strong woman, just like you, Fey. You both have this… intuition I admire. I think you'd get along with her if you gave her the chance."

A strong woman. Just like me.

Just then, something buzzed past Fey's ear. She brushed it

away, but it came back to hover in her face. Frankie shot a look at the fly.

Why do Frankie's eyes look like that?

Frankie swatted at the fly, narrowly missing Fey's nose. The buzzing stopped and Fey watched as it spiraled in the air, to the backseat. There, it landed on the clay pot and dizzily tried to regain its footing.

Fey watched as it crawled from the rim of the pot toward one of the open mouths. The fly tapped its feet over the plant's teeth and into the center of the mouth. Its wings flitted one last time and Fey watched the plant close itself over it.

The fly was gone. No more.

The Covista trap just ate it up.

Fey grasped onto her wet book, hoping its pages weren't completely ruined.

"Well, look at that." Frankie's voice broke through Fey's thoughts. Her eyes were back to their cheerful blue color. "It looks like it might be slowin' down."

Sure enough, the rain had trimmed down to almost nothing. The storm was moving on as quickly as it had arrived.

"You better get on out of this car before it picks back up again or you'll end up washin' away down the street." Frankie unlocked the car doors and shooed her hand at Fey. "Go on. Shoo! Get yourself in that house and dry off."

Fey pulled the door handle to let herself out. As she watched Frankie reverse out of her driveway, she hugged her book tight. When Frankie reached the road, she rolled down a window and stuck her hand out. "Don't forget the bag from Claire tomorrow!" A single red curl dropped in front of her eyes.

Fey unlocked her front door and slid herself inside. "I'm home, Fern," she called out. It hung in the window, looming over her, reminding her of the same warning she told herself daily.

Stay out of the forest.

She walked past Fern and placed her book down to dry. She didn't want to hear it right now. No. She was going to face those damned woods. She just needed some help to find the right spot.

Frankie was the right person to help her with that.

CHAPTER SEVEN

One Year + Four Months Earlier

Bruce's hand felt like a comforting puzzle piece, his fingers intertwining with Fey's in perfect placement. She nuzzled against his arm and felt his warmth spread to her as they made their way down Main Street.

The sidewalk was full of elbows and shoulders bumping into Fey's side. None of these nameless strangers bothered to apologize or step aside. They were too busy burying their noses into their phones or clutching their shopping bags full of designer clothes in fear.

Everyone is so damned concerned with themselves.

They passed by coffee shops with unpronounceable drink names, a corner-side street florist with overpriced roses plucked straight from a delivery truck miles away, and a hipster bar full of loud music and flashing lights. Each building was a cluttered chaos Fey hated. She longed for a community where people focused on connection with people rather than with materialism.

"Let's go in here, Honey Pot." Bruce pointed to a tech store filled with gadgets illuminated by tiny spotlights.

Fey clenched her fingers around his arm.

She could predict what he was going to say next. *I just wanna fiddle with buttons.*

"I just wanna fiddle with buttons."

"Sure," she said through gritted teeth. She hated these walks through the crowds, but swallowed her angst as long as she had his arm to grasp.

They walked into the shop together. It sounded off in beeps and clicks from all the display devices on the tables. It was like they were all chattering in a language Fey didn't understand. It made her skin crawl.

"Hi. Can I help you find anything today? What brings you in?"

A store employee greeted them in less time than it took to take two steps through the door. She gave Bruce a squeeze, hoping he would stay by her side but knowing better. He would want to follow the associate down the aisles and engage in a conversation that would excite his fixation. And she would rather meander away from anyone pressuring her to buy until he was ready to leave.

Fey reached in her pocket and fished out a stick of gum. With her nerves pushed aside, she wandered off to see if she could find something to occupy her mind. She perused the tables, trailing a finger mindlessly in front of each display. Watches that controlled the thermostat, keyboards that folded to fit in your pocket, sunglasses with built-in Bluetooth speakers.

Why the hell would anyone want speakers on their spectacles?

It was all the same to her: non-necessities sold under the guise of convenience.

She glanced up at Bruce. He was still talking to the same employee in the kitchen section. They were in front of an herb planter. From where she stood, she saw a light that mimicked the sun's changing colors throughout the day. As Bruce pressed a button, Fey heard it beep. A screen in front of the plants displayed a happy face. The emoji opened its mouth and happily accepted a digital piece of food.

Great. Just what everyone needs. A digital way to feed kitchen plants.

She hugged herself tight, hoping Bruce would hurry up. As she rubbed her arms, she looked down to find herself in front of a large monitor. It was full of dirty fingerprints from several customers touching it throughout the day. Fey shuddered at the thought of how many dirty hands touched the screen in front of her.

But something caught her eye. Past the dirty fingerprints was a map displayed on the screen. Someone must have left it up after messing with the apps, only to mess with some other screen with some other buttons. It reminded her of the maps inside the front cover of fantasy books. Fey loved when authors included one in their novels. It both withheld and hastened consumption of the actual story. Maps like that filled her with anxious anticipation. She always knew there was a full story to digest within its fictional town surrounded by mystical woods.

This, though, was no fantasy-based map. The *Google Maps* icon was proof. This was real. She recognized Saint Paign smack dab in the middle with its cluttered streets. The highways twisted in knots around the city's center and secondary roads branched off like spider webs.

As her eyes shifted away from the familiar clutter, she realized there was more to the map. There, in the far north corner of the map, was proof more existed outside of the city she always knew. A small town was carved away with a forest accompanying it.

I'll be damned. A fictional town, and surrounded by mystical woods.

Her heart raced. Here was a real-life map telling her there could be the exact opposite of the agitation she's always known. It was right there in front of her, waiting to tell her a full-length story of its own. If she could close her eyes, she could imagine the possibilities awaiting in this tiny little secret town she had never noticed before.

"Can I interest you in the next model up, ma'am? It's got a higher resolution and twice the durability than the one in front of you!"

The hell?

"What? No." Fey shook her head. "Actually, could you tell me what this is?" She pointed to the northern corner of the map.

"Let's see… oh, that? It's a tiny town up north. I think it's called Soura… something. Someone came in earlier talking about it. He pulled it up, mentioned something about driving through on a business trip soon, and left it there. That's all."

Soura. Soura...what?

Fey realized somewhere in her daze, she had stopped chewing her gum. She moved her jaw again and absorbed the last bit of flavor left.

"You sure I can't show you the next model up?"

"What? Oh, no. I'm good," Fey replied without looking up. She continued to stare into this little unknown town. How had she gone her whole life without knowing what was waiting for her outside of her hometown?

"You said someone talked to you about it earlier?" She looked up at the associate, who seemed irritated with her disinterest.

"Yeah. Some guy. He said he was going to swing through the place on the way back from his next business trip or something. I don't know. There are a lot of people who come in here and I can't keep up with all their stories. I'd never make a buck if I did. Listen lady, if you're not going to buy it, I'm going to go help a customer who actually needs my help."

What could this mysterious place be like? She imagined it was a place anyone would feel welcome, a place where you couldn't get lost in a sea of a bunch of 'someones' and 'somethings', a place where people focused on people and connections and the values that actually mattered.

She pictured Mom and Pop shops lining a street, each owned by a town resident. She pictured comfortable houses, not too big and not too small, peppered along secondary roads. She pictured cobblestone and smiling faces and the smell of freshly baked apple pie...

"Ready, Honey Pot?"

Bruce's ridiculous pet name woke Fey out of her daydreaming.

"Yeah, sure. Let's go." Fey allowed Bruce to pull her away from the map so she could resume her position, hand in his, nuzzled against his arm, chewing lightly on her gum.

"Did you see the watches they had in there? And the kitchen stuff? They have something for everything, like a programmable coffee grinder! I know how much you like your coffee. One day, Fey... one day I'll get you that grinder and anything else you need in there."

A programmable coffee pot is just fine. Who the hell needs to grind their beans when you can buy grounds by the pound?

Fey squeezed his hand tightly.

He squeezed hers right back. "I know you think I'm crazy, Fey, but I'm not. Some day, you'll have to stop being thankful for the scraps that get us by. Our tiny apartment? The beat up car? A minimum wage job? It's okay for right now, but you deserve so much more. And one day, I'll make it happen. You deserve to have some luxuries in life, including that coffee grinder."

A minty scent escaped Fey's mouth as she exhaled.

"Are you chewing gum again?" Bruce sighed heavily. "You know that tears apart your teeth, right?"

Fey rolled her eyes, but dropped her gum in a nearby trash can.

The luxuries of life.
She laughed to herself.
What the hell does that even mean?

Back at their apartment, Fey and Bruce sat down to a microwavable pot pie. Even though it was still cold in the middle, Bruce ate it with gusto.

"Mmmm, Honey Pot. You know how to feed a man at the end of the day."

Fey poked at her own plate and wished she didn't fear cooking in the oven. Every time she thought about trying, she pictured the oven exploding, catching their home on fire.

"Bruce, do you think it's time I look through one of the cookbooks collecting dust on the shelf? This seems so preposterous to rely on the microwave to do all the cooking for us."

Bruce raised an eyebrow. "You sure you want to do that, Honey Pot?"

Dropping her fork on her plate, Fey walked over to the bookshelf and found a cookbook. The cover pictured a casserole dish dressed with curly green leaves. She flipped open to a page that read, **Chicken Pot Pie**.

"See? I could assemble one of these." She scanned the directions on the page. "Only, this is a lot of steps. There's a lot that could go wrong." Fey felt her stomach churn as she took a bite of the pot pie on her plate. "And this isn't so bad. It's safe, right?"

Bruce shoved a heaping fork of food into his mouth and

chewed in an overly animated way. "Mmmm!" He rubbed his belly and took a second heaping bite. "Honey Pot, you don't need to cook any differently. This is delicious just as it is."

Dinner went silent after that. Once they'd emptied their plates, Fey cleaned up, wondering if she would ever face her fear of the kitchen. When it came to food, she wanted to keep it as safe as possible. There were too many ways she could screw up a good meal. Forget burning or overcooking. She was more worried about a kitchen appliance catching fire or undercooked chicken making them sick. No; a pretty dressed-up pot pie wasn't worth it. She'd stick to what was safest.

As Fey washed and put away the last dish, her shoulder brushed against something. Startled, she jumped. Then she realized what it was.

Fern.

Her heart rate sped up. Even though she forgot about the plant hanging in the window, Fern wouldn't allow her to forget for long. There it was, hovering over her shoulder, watching her every move.

Fey backed out of the kitchen away from the plant and into the living room. There was Bruce, on the couch, with a Chuck Norris movie on the T.V.

"You must realize the greatest weapon you possess is self-control."

Sidekicks. Fey had most of the dialogue memorized.

As Bruce karate-chopped into the air, Fey replaced the cookbook she wasn't going to cook from back on the bookshelf. Instead, she scanned for something else. A brown cover stuck out a little further than the rest of the books. **A history of Saint Paign**. She pulled it out along with a Moleskine notebook.

Settling herself next to Bruce, she flipped the pages. She stopped when she found a full page map. A map that looked eerily similar to the one in the store earlier. Instantly, she looked at the top corner of the page.

Soura Heights. So that's the name of the small town.

Fey liked it. It sounded quiet and quaint. It sounded like the kind of place where people valued people and not their shopping bags and cell phones.

Bruce made another karate chop.

In her Moleskine notebook, Fey copied the name of the small town at the top of a clean page. For the length of the movie, she wrote until her hand cramped up. She dreamt of how Soura Heights would be the exact opposite of the chaos she was used to. It was a place with cobblestone roads and Mom and Pop shops. It was a place where people valued relationships instead of their phones. A place where she could escape when Saint Paign became too much.

When the movie credits rolled, Fey shut her journal. Soura Heights felt like storybook perfection. It was too good to be true.

CHAPTER EIGHT

Present Day

The next day's weather in Soura Heights returned to its normal, sunshiny demeanor. Puffy white clouds hung above Fey and the air smelled freshly clean. If it weren't for the collection of puddles on the sidewalk, no one would have ever known it rained like it did.

Fey filled her lungs with the fresh air in front of A Pair of Dice Lost.

"Hi, Miss Davis."

Miss Davis responded with a grunt.

Fey helped herself to the shelves. Yesterday's weather made her eager to find a book that wasn't soaked through the covers.

Fey's guilt about the wet book at home ate up her thinking. Allowing rain to ruin the bit of help she hoped for Fern felt like a bad omen.

Fey's finger found a book with an orange spine. Intrigued, she pulled it out and looked on the cover. Front and center was a tan house cat with a mouth full of long, green blades of grass. Its mouth was open, displaying sharp, pointed teeth.

Like a miniature mountain lion.

Fey shuddered as she read the title out loud. "Plants That Kill Us."

Damned plants.

Miss Davis grunted behind her.

"I know, Miss Davis. No reading in the store. I'll buy it."

Fey tucked the book under her arm. On the same shelf, she found a cookbook and grabbed that, too. Miss Davis waved her out the door.

Fey breathed in the fresh air again. Some days, she felt like she was in a fairy tale. Other days, she wasn't sure if that were the case. Yesterday's storm felt like she could have been drifting into something far more sinister than Goldilocks or Rapunzel.

She found Claire and her daughter side by side on the bench in front of You Herb It Here First.

Damn it. I forgot Frankie's bag again.

Guilt rose up in her throat. Her mouth tasted sour. She bit her lip in self-punishment for being so forgetful. Fey thought about going back home for it, but stopped when she noticed BettyAnne's lap. Her tiny hand was stroking a cat.

Didn't a cat meow before the storm?

Unlike the book cover, this didn't look like a tiny mountain lion. It didn't even look like a beloved pet. This cat looked rough and ragged. Its pink skin peeked through where its fur was missing. The black patches that were left looked matted and scabbed over. Fey could hear BettyAnne's tiny voice crack in a whisper. "It's okay, kitty. It's okay."

The cat flopped over BettyAnne's lap as if it were sick of the world around it. Claire's arm engulfed the five-year-old in a feeble attempt at soothing her. Claire looked up at Fey and gave her a pitiful half-smile. "Hi Fey. Did you need to pick up something for Frankie?"

Fey shook her head and bit her lip again. Then, she realized how close she was to Claire and BettyAnne. She must have looked like she was hovering over them. "No, I don't-"

Claire looked confused. "Did June place an order?"

"No."

"Okay. Well, is there anything else I can help you with?"

Fey shook her head again. Claire rubbed BettyAnne's back in repetitive circles. The little girl was still petting the cat on her lap, trying to heal it from its misery. Fey had the feeling she was intruding on a sensitive situation. She turned to step away from their moment, then Claire carefully stood up from her bench.

"Wait," she said. "Can I talk to you a minute?"

Fey stopped in her tracks. "Sure." She clutched her books in her arms.

Claire walked Fey a few steps away, leaving their backs facing BettyAnne alone with the cat. "I'm glad you came by, Fey!" Her voice was cheerful, unwavering, assuring her daughter there was no need for worry. Then, she leaned in closer and spoke in a hushed tone.

"I have no idea what to do, Fey. No idea."

Fey looked over at BettyAnne. The poor girl's face was stained with tears.

Claire continued. "I've never been much of a pet person, let alone a cat person. But that girl of mine? Her heart is soft for them. She has always wanted one of her own. She's always said if I let her have a cat, she would take care of it by herself. She would feed it, brush it, play with it, and so forth. But I always knew I wouldn't have the time or energy for a cat. Being a mom and shopkeeper keeps me exhausted as it is." Claire looked frustrated at the thought of a pet. "But just look at her. Look at that pitiful face."

Both women looked behind them. Claire's expression softened as she watched BettyAnne. She had stopped stroking the cat's fur and was inspecting one of the bald spots behind its ear.

"She found that cat behind the store about 15 minutes ago. The sitter dropped her off so she could play around in the breakroom before closing for lunch hours, but she got distracted when she heard this sad little meow."

Fey remembered the meow she had heard the day before. The meow that announced a storm.

Or was it a meow that called for help?

"She followed it and found it, just laying there balding and weak. It must be a stray, I guess. There's no collar or tag or anything. And it's not well. It's not good. Just look at it." Again, Claire gestured to the bench. "What am I supposed to do with it? I know nothing about cats, let alone how to take care of a sick stray. BettyAnne just won't part with it now she has it on her lap. She would be devastated if it died on us, you know? Do you know anything about cats? Please?" Claire looked hopefully at Fey, waiting for a helpful offering.

Fey looked at her book in her hand. *Plants That Kill Us.*

"I-I... Is it okay?" was all Fey could manage.

"I don't think so. It's such a pitiful looking thing. It doesn't sound good, either. And I know BettyAnne can sense that, too. Oh, the poor girl is just going to be heartbroken if we can't help it. Gosh, what do I do?"

65

Fey thought back to a conversation she once had with Frankie. As a child, Frankie took in a stray cat even though her dad was allergic and vowed to keep their home feline-free.

"Let me go get Frankie..." Fey turned to walk toward the pie shop, her gut wrenching.

"No, wait!" Claire called back at her. "Please. I can't do this alone."

Fey stopped. She looked at the cover of her book again. "Do you think it ate something it shouldn't have?"

Claire's eyes widened. "What if it did? How would I know? Oh Fey, what do I do?"

Just then, June walked by. Fey barely recognized her from her short haircut. Her stoic gait gave her away.

"Hey June!" Fey called out.

June stopped in her tracks. She held something in her hands— a potted plant?

A damned flytrap.

Fey felt her mouth go dry as she remembered the flytrap in Frankie's car. She shook off the growing feeling. "June. Could you ask Frankie to lend us her assistance? We could benefit from her experience."

Instantly, Fey felt a twinge of embarrassment. June's eyebrow raised. "You need Frankie's help."

"Mommy. The kitty is making a funny noise." BettyAnne's hands stopped moving. She wearily looked up at Claire, hoping for an explanation. It didn't sound like a meow. It wasn't as loud as when Fey heard it before. It was like a low growl, but weak and gurgly.

Fey gave June a desperate look. "Yes, please."

She watched June disappear down the cobblestone road, hoping she would bring back Frankie and free her from this situation.

Claire spoke through gritted teeth, "Are you sure Frankie knows about these things?"

Fey could only shrug her shoulders. She had no idea if Frankie would know what to do, but Frankie's confidence would be a better fit for this situation than Fey's mousey temperament, even if she didn't.

As they waited, Fey noticed the plaid shirt man across the

street. He was standing in the shade of a tree, with his phone in hand, outstretched. Fey assumed he was taking photos and she rolled her eyes. If she had any doubt before, now she was sure he was an out-of-towner. A hand on her elbow broke her concentration.

"Take extra care of a moggie's bare cast."

"Hi, Louise."

Louise moved her shaky hand away from Fey and over to the cat. She left it hovering over its fur without touching it.

"Don't let the red fox feed it. A lynx would do better if she knew how."

As quietly as she arrived, the old lady disappeared. With frightened eyes, BettyAnne looked up at Claire. "Mommy, why did the witch say that?"

Claire brushed BettyAnne's hair behind her ears. "Oh honey, I've told you before. Ms. Louise isn't a witch. She's just old and lonely. She doesn't know what she's saying." She gave the little girl a kiss on the head. "Don't you worry. Ms. Frankie will be here soon to help, okay?"

Claire looked back at Fey and again asked through tight lips, "Where is she? Is she coming soon?"

Five minutes felt like an eternity, but Frankie finally arrived outside the herb shop. "It's a slow day for pies, ladies. What's up?"

Claire gestured over to BettyAnne and the moaning cat on her lap.

"Oh, I see." Frankie smiled and inched over to the bench. She sat down next to BettyAnne and placed her arm around the little girl. "Hi, BettyAnne. Remember me?" Her voice soothed the strained air between the group. Fey didn't realize she had been clenching her jaw until Frankie's voice relaxed her.

BettyAnne nodded her head, slowly.

"Good. So, we're friends, right? Say, what do you have there?"

"A kitty." The little girl's voice was even tinier than before, sadder. Her tone mimicked the cat's suffering meow.

"I see that. And where did you find the kitty?"

BettyAnne pointed her little finger to the back of the building.

"She found it like that. The poor thing looks awful, doesn't it?" Claire was nearly biting her nails.

The cat made the weird gurgling sound again.

Sounds awful, too.

Frankie put her hand on the back of the cat's neck, stroking what was left of its fur. "It's okay, BettyAnne. You know, I had a kitty just like this when I was little."

"You did?"

Fey listened closely to hear any details she may have missed in her memory.

"Yup. Her name was Boots. I was just about your age when I found her wanderin' outside. Maybe a little older. After all, an old lady like me can't remember everythin' exactly." She elbowed BettyAnne in jest. The little girl let out a quiet giggle. She was relaxing, too. "I named her Boots because she had these tiny white paws that looked like boots." Frankie held her hand on the cat's neck. She gazed down on it in a pensive manner. "My daddy didn't really like cats much. He was allergic, kept sneezin' every time he was around Boots." She briefly paused, then smiled at BettyAnne. "I think I know just the thing for this kitty. Does he have a name?"

BettyAnne thought for a moment. "Patches. Because of his fur."

Fey thought she could see Frankie's hand tighten on Patches's neck. Her eyes looked funny again. Their blue color had drained, leaving behind dark holes for irises. Patches didn't make a sound. He accepted being under Frankie's grip.

Frankie smiled again at BettyAnne. "Patches, huh? That sounds like a great name for him. Well, I tell you what, BettyAnne. How about I take Patches with me and see what I can do, huh?"

The little girl looked unsure, worried. "What are you going to do with him?"

"Oh see. Boots was sick, too, when I had her. But my daddy taught me what I needed to do with sick kitties. He walked me through every bit of the way to take care of Boots so she wouldn't be sick anymore." Patches made a quietly rough sound as Frankie lifted him up and onto her own lap.

"Really? You're going to make Patches better?"

"I can do everythin' my daddy taught me," Frankie assured BettyAnne. "Don't you worry a bit. Why don't you go home with mommy and I'll take care of the rest, okay?" She blinked and her eyes were blue again. Fey blinked her eyes, too. Again, her vision was playing tricks on her.

Claire looked relieved as Frankie carried Patches away. "Thank you so much, Frankie. You have no idea how happy you've made my little girl. I guess we need to pick up some pet supplies to welcome home our new family member. I can't thank you enough!"

Frankie stopped mid-step. She held onto Patches, who was no longer making any noise. Without looking over her shoulder, she spoke loudly enough for only the adults to hear. "I wouldn't bother shoppin', Claire." Without another word, she continued to walk away toward the pie shop.

A little while later, Fey found herself sitting in a booth. June placed a slice of plain apple pie in front of her. Fey noticed June's hands were clean, though her nails hid a small amount of caked dirt under them.

Did she pull that damned plant up today?

As June left her table, Fey stole a look at the front desk. Next to the clear canisters of tea was a terracotta pot. The Covista Trap had found its home. Frankie emerged from the back room and Fey watched her pass her table and make her way to the plant. She pulled something out of her apron pocket—a vial?

What the hell is that?

With her other hand, she reached back into her apron pocket and pulled out a pair of tweezers. In horror, Fey watched as Frankie opened the vial and reached in with tweezers.

Inside, a round black bug scurried away from her grasp. It tried crawling up the glass side, but it slid back down, several legs flailing.

With precision, Frankie pinched the bug with the tweezers and pulled it out. Fey's mouth grew sour as she saw the tweezers lower toward the fly trap. Frankie let go when the plant's mouth closed over it.

Fey swallowed and pushed her plate aside. She didn't have an appetite anymore.

Frankie dropped her tools back in her apron and brushed her hands clean. Before Fey knew it, Frankie was sitting in front of her, wearing her typical smile, her red curls dropping in her face.

"How's Patches?" Fey asked before Frankie could say a word.

"Not even a 'hello', huh?" Frankie's tone was playful. "Just 'How's the cat?'"

Fey tried again, "Hi, Frankie."

"That's more like it! Hello to you, too, Buttercup! Want to go over birthday plans? Only two days to go before the big two-one!"

Frankie leaned an elbow on the table.

Fey sighed deeply. She wasn't in the mood to go over any birthday details. "No... I just-"

"Geeze, Fey, you only turn 21 once. You think a girl would want to make it a mark worth rememberin'. Do I have to do all the plannin' for you?"

"I just wanted to know... how's Patches?"

Now it was Frankie's turn to sigh. "You didn't seriously come here to ask about that cat, did you?"

"BettyAnne seemed pretty upset..."

"Gosh, you are being way too sensitive. Yeah. She's a kid. Kids get upset. They get upset over everythin'."

"But, Frankie, Patches seemed-"

"That cat was sick, Fey. Sick. Did you see its hair fallin' out? Did you hear the noises it was makin'? It was sick." Frankie looked at the books Fey stacked on the table. She pointed to the picture with the cat. "It probably ate somethin' it shouldn't have. Claire dumps all kinds of expired herbs into the trash out back—oregano, bay leaves, tarragon—I'd be willin' to bet any one of those would be poison to a desperately hungry wanderin' cat."

"Didn't your dad show you how to help sick cats?"

"Fey, Daddy took care of Boots. That cat was sick and unhappy. Daddy said if it kept on, it would get worse and the cat would just die a slow death. But Daddy took care of it a lot quicker. It

70

wasn't slow at all. Within a few minutes, that cat wasn't sick anymore and I didn't have to worry about it. Sure, as a kid, I was upset. But I got over it. And BettyAnne will, too."

Was Frankie admitting to something without giving an outright confession? Was she insinuating her father killed her beloved childhood pet? As an adult, was she okay with that now?

Frankie's eyes blinked back their color. "Enough about cats and kids. Let's chat about birthdays! I want to do somethin' amazin' for you. After all, it's also a pretty big anniversary, moving out here on your own. I think you deserve to have some kind of celebration. A celebration of the strong woman you are."

Fey opened her mouth. She wanted to ask about the forest.

Covista Forest. The Covista Trap.

But nothing came out.

"I tell you what, you don't have to worry about it." Frankie brushed the curls away from her eyes. "I'll take care of it all. Buckle up, Buttercup."

Fey grimaced as Frankie reached back in her apron pocket. She didn't want to see another bug in a vial. To her relief, Frankie pulled out one of Claire's brown bags. Frankie's fingers pulled something out and sprinkled it on top of Fey's untouched plate. "Candied pecans. Things always taste so much better when they're dressed up a little."

With that, she left the table and called over her shoulder, "Oh and don't forget to bring me that order you picked up from Claire!"

Even with a pretty topping, Fey's appetite was still gone. She gathered her books, hugged them close, and left Pie-Pie For Now without a bite.

All the way home, she tried to shake off the feeling that something was wrong. As she reached the clothing shop, she stopped in front of the display window. Again, the polo shirt stared at her. A wave of nausea washed over her and she tasted bile wretching from her stomach. Just enough to fill her mouth and spit onto the ground.

She left it and the polo shirt behind her and walked toward home, Covista Forest waiting for her in the distance.

71

CHAPTER NINE

One Year + Three Months Earlier

"Do you see the yard on that one?" Bruce pointed out the window to a two-story Colonial with black shutters and a yellow front door. The park-like front yard displayed two benches facing each other in front of a rose garden with a climbing trellis.

"Oh, and look at that one over there! How many cars do you think that garage could hold?" On the other side of the street was a matching house with gray shutters. The build was exactly the same, except there was added space above a garage large enough for, Fey guessed, three vehicles, four if they were compact.

"Oh wow, Fey! What do you think that extra building is for?" The driveway Bruce pointed to forked, leading two opposite directions. To the left was a two-story house with a green door. To the right, a miniature version of the main house with the same green door, large enough to have its own mortgage attached to it.

Every house on Mercury Lane was like this; a cookie-cutter build, field-like yards, and enough space for a ten-person family, even though none of the families were large enough to utilize the space they had.

Superfluous twats.

This was Bruce's idea of a fun evening. He wanted to draw out a future in one of these Mercury Lane homes with a white picket fence and too much land for the two of them plus Fern.

"Aren't these homes… garishly showy?"

"Garishly…? Fey, no. They're beautiful! Just imagine calling one home!"

She did. She didn't like it. A home like that meant values were thrown to the far corners of a house too large. It was space she could feel lost in. Fey grabbed Bruce's hand as he drove slowly down the street. She didn't want to get lost in anything but him.

Fey sighed heavily as her husband continued to point out

house after house in idolization. Even though there wasn't a single person watching them from their yards, she could feel the judgment behind the closed windows. He must have caught on to her silent discomfort because he stopped asking about the yards. He stopped pointing out the driveways. And he stopped admiring the wrap-around porches. He placed both hands on the wheel and quietly turned the car around, leaving the collective Mercury homes behind.

Fey felt the tension in the car swell. She looked over at Bruce. His jawline was tight from clenching his teeth.

She quietly took a deep breath. "Are you okay?" she asked softly. "I thought-"

"Well, *I* thought we were having a great drive out together."

"We were-" Fey tried to put her hand on his knee, but he shook it free.

"No. *I* was, Fey. You... you clearly weren't." His knuckles tightened on the steering wheel.

"I was--"

"Fey, you've barely said a word since I started up the car. You've been staring out into space as if there was somewhere else you'd rather be."

Fey looked down at her hands on her lap. There wasn't anywhere else she'd rather be, not really. There certainly wasn't anyone else she'd rather be with. She just didn't know how to share the interest in adoring a home she didn't need in a town she didn't love.

"Is there?"

"Huh?" Fey looked at him, confused.

"Is there somewhere else you'd rather be?"

"No." Fey did her best to convince him in a single syllable.

Bruce turned at a stoplight a road away from their apartment. The whites on his knuckles were still there. "Well then, what is it? Because you're certainly not bursting with excitement." His voice sounded bothered, annoyed by her presence in the car. "Or maybe your head is with one of those books of yours." The disdain grew in his tone.

He continued to drive in silence, rolling into a stop at the stop sign before turning into the apartment complex's parking lot. Parking in his designated spot, Bruce cut the ignition, but didn't get up. Fey kept to her seat even after she unbuckled her seatbelt. She stared at their weathered apartment door in front of them. The black number 329 was aged with rust. The blue paint on the door chipped at the edges. It was just as worn as their little Jeep, and probably had more stories within its walls than any of the houses on Mercury Lane.

Bruce tapped his thumb on the steering wheel and bit his bottom lip. Finally, he turned to her. "Fey. I think you need to get out. Go inside."

"But-"

"Stop. I don't want to talk to you right now. You're clearly not talking to me and it's getting us nowhere. I need some air."

Fey hesitantly opened the passenger side door and let herself out. She turned around to close it, but Bruce had already leaned over the seat to take care of it. He drove away without even a wave.

Fey was dumbfounded. Never before had she seen Bruce upset, let alone been the cause of it. It was astounding how quickly he went from his bubbly personality to a stern calm. This wasn't the Bruce she knew; at least, she had never seen this side of him. It worried her. Did she say something wrong?

No. He was prompt to point that out. I didn't say enough.

Fey wrapped her arms around herself and squeezed a rigid hug. Then, she unlocked the front door. It was weird walking into the apartment by herself. It was empty except for Fern in the corner, who beckoned for a watering, and it was quiet except for the muffled shuffling from the renters in the apartment above.

Her Moleskine notebook waited on the dining table. She opened it to the last page she wrote in. At the top of the page, she wrote **A Slice of Soura**—a placeholder for a better title later.

For an hour, she put ink to paper, writing about leaving behind a frivolous lifestyle for a close-knit community. The way she wrote about Soura Heights, it was everything opposite of Saint Paign. Excess wasn't a thought. It was a place where she would *fit*, where things would make sense. Fey was sure this was where she would want to be.

Fey took a break to stretch her back and crack her knuckles. She looked out the front door into the parking lot. Bruce was still gone, still getting his air.

She shuffled back over to the table but left her notebook alone. Writing for herself felt wrong. She was guilty for enjoying it when she should be fretting over Bruce.

I need a nap.

Fey helped herself to the bedroom and laid down without pulling back the sheets. Maybe Bruce would be home by the time she opened her eyes again.

Just a minute.

Fey's catnap turned into a small hibernation. Having no idea how long she had been asleep, she rubbed her eyes awake. From the other room, she heard... what did she hear?

Is that... paper?

Bruce was home.

Is Bruce home?

She had thought she would have found him curled next to her in bed. Or if not in bed, at least she would have thought he would have been on the couch with Chuck Norris on the T.V. in front of him. But the only sound she heard sounded like pages turning.

What the hell?

She shifted her weight off the bed, wrinkling the sheets from under her. Afraid to draw attention to herself, she tiptoed across the room. If Bruce wasn't curled up next to her or in his usual place on the couch, maybe he was still irritated.

Fey cracked open the bedroom door and peered out into the living room. There, Bruce was at the table, her Moleskine notebook in hand. As the bedroom door creaked open, Bruce's eyes looked up, peering over the cover's edge. His mouth was agape.

"Fey...I..." He looked back at the book, trying to find words to say. "I'm so sorry."

She took another step toward him and shrugged her shoulders. "It's okay."

Is it okay? Why the hell does he have my notebook?

"Come here." Bruce stood up from his chair and offered his

arms outward. There was no sign of the antagonized man she was in the car with earlier. Now, there was only the same Bruce she had ever known in front of her. She accepted his offer and fell into his body, allowing her weight to push against his chest. Even still, there was something in her that felt hesitant. He nuzzled her as he apologized again. "I'm sorry, Fey. I had no idea."

No idea about what?

She allowed herself to feel him exhale against her neck. Somehow, it felt new, as if she had never felt his breath on her skin before. She concentrated on matching her breathing pattern until she fell in sync with his.

He whispered in her ear. "Fey, why didn't you tell me?"

"Tell you what?"

Bruce moved himself away from her, pushing her shoulders off his chest. He gestured toward the face-down notebook, his mouth wide. "This, Fey. This."

She picked it up to see where he had left off. It was the last page she left off on. The last word was in dark pen, underlined with intent.

Perfection.

As in, **Life where people valued benevolence over possession was sheer perfection**.

She cringed while reading her own written words.

"Fey, you know I'm your biggest fan when it comes to your writing." He paused briefly and pointed to the open page in front of her. "And this? This is your best work, yet. I can tell, this is more than just a fluff story for kicks. This? This is you, isn't it?"

What the hell is that supposed to mean?

Fey bit her inner lip. Enough to draw blood.

How... Why did he read it? I never asked him to.

"It is. It's you. I'm so sorry about earlier. I just wanted so bad for you to want what *I* wanted. I wanted you to want to be with me. I wanted you to want one of those crazy big houses, maybe not now, but one day in our future. I wanted you to *want* to daydream with me about what that might look like for us." He sat down again, gesturing to her handwriting. "But I didn't stop to ask about what it is *you* actually wanted."

Fey breathed out heavily. "It's not finished."

"Oh, I know it's not finished, Fey. It's not finished because *you're* not finished. The way you describe this place, this Soura Heights, I can tell you have an affection for it. Is it real? Is there really a small town like this somewhere you want to go?"

Fey blushed. Through gritted teeth, she said, "It's real. At least, sort of."

"What do you mean, 'sort of'?"

"Soura Heights. It's a real place. I saw it on a map once and it just seemed so..." Fey had a hard time finding a single word to describe how the town that was half-real and half-made up made her feel.

"Perfect. It says so right here." Bruce pointed at the last handwritten word. "Your words, not mine." He shrugged.

It's. Not. Finished.

"Sure, perfect," she said through pursed lips. It wasn't fair that Bruce could point out her own words to her when she couldn't easily find them herself. "But, it's not."

"Explain."

Fey took a breath. "I made it all up. It's just fiction. There's nothing really true about it other than the name. It's Alice's Wonderland." The mention of another favorite book made the words trickle out easier. "When I close my eyes and I think of Soura Heights, it becomes something of a Wonderland itself. It's nothing like our world here in Saint Paign. It's like I can just feel this humble little town take over. I can hear the shop owners' voices. I can feel the stone paths under my feet. I can feel the open air, like when we go to Salt Point, but better. It feels cleaner. It feels clearer. It's relaxing, Bruce, not like Saint Paign."

"You're not happy here? You're not relaxed?"

"How can I be? Everywhere you turn, you bump into a stranger's elbow, overhear their conversations of infidelity, or smell the burnt coffee on their breath as you pass them by." Just then, the upstairs neighbors shut a bedroom door. The slight *thud* echoed from the ceiling above them. Fey pointed up. "See what I mean? There's more noise than there is space."

Bruce shrugged his shoulders. "But that's why we were over at Mercury. One day, we won't be in this apartment. We won't be able to hear the neighbors through thin walls. We will have all the space we could need."

She shook her head at him. "It's not just the apartment, Bruce. It's this whole damn place!" She spread her arms out, almost knocking over a glass of water on the table. "The whole city is like an expanded version of our apartment. No one waves hello down the street. No one knows your name unless they're running your credit card through a machine. No one makes any effort to get to know anyone else. People work themselves to the bone and spend the money they earn on the next thing to sink themselves into, letting their brains rot away on the materialistic nonsense. No one actually cares about anyone else. It's maddening. It's all a robotic means to a mechanical end."

Bruce grabbed her by the arm. "Is that what you think?" She could feel his hand getting tighter, tight enough to leave red imprints on her skin. He yanked her close to him, handling her harder than he ever had before. She could see his arms tensing up again and wondered if he was going to white knuckle her arm the same way he did with the steering wheel. It scared her.

What is he doing?

He grabbed her by the other arm, just as tight. Then, he leaned in and kissed her hard, harder than he ever had before. At first, Fey pulled away, unsure how to react. Then her muscles grew limp as she relaxed into him to kiss back. The shock that ran through her body reminded her, this, being with Bruce, this was home. Bruce was home. Right now in this moment, the butterflies that lived in her stopped beating their wings. They held their movement as she held her breath. Nothing else mattered. Her frustration with Saint Paign, her writing, their argument, it was all just chaff that stood still. Now, it was just her and Bruce, and he was more home to her than ever.

She felt his hands move from her arms to the small of her back. Her body naturally pressed into his and their breaths grew heavy together. As she contemplated if he tasted more like cream or milk, she opened her eyes. She felt herself falling forward and his chair leaning back. Unable to correct their balance in time, they fell together off their chairs and onto the carpeted floor. They had fallen hard, side by side, their legs half under the table they were just sitting at.

Fey started to laugh; so did Bruce. The ridiculousness hit them both just as hard as they had hit the floor. Lying together, he held her next to him, his arm cradling her shoulder. "Are you okay?" he asked, chuckling quietly.

She wrapped her arm over his chest to hold him. "I'm okay. Are you?" She slowed her laugh enough to look up at his eyes.

He moved a hand up to his head and rubbed the side. "I hit my head a little, but I think I'll be okay."

Fey smiled. "Bruce."

"Yeah?"

"Soura Heights isn't really real. It's just a Wonderland; part of my imagination. The connection you saw in there? It's pretend. This right here is the real connection." She hugged him tight. "Even if we're in a crowd of millions, I'm okay as long as you promise to kiss me like that again." She loved that with every passing day, she continued to build connections with her husband. That was the real deal. In Saint Paign, in Soura Heights, hell, even in a ditch off of Mercury Road... this was what she ached for.

Bruce laughed and kissed her again, gentler, slower this time. When he broke away, he nuzzled her neck. "Fey, I'll kiss you like that every day for the rest of my life as long as you'll let me." He looked around at the floor next to them. A fractured piece of wood lay splintered off to the side. The chair he fell from broke a leg. "But there's just one thing..."

Fey fell into his nuzzling and pulled herself closer into him. "What's that?"

He rubbed his head again. "As long as we don't end up falling like this again. I don't know if I could handle another bump to my head."

CHAPTER TEN

Present Day

Fey woke up the next morning, the thought of Patches a faded memory. She made herself a morning coffee and sat in her oversized chair by the window. She took a sip of the dark roast and savored its warm bitterness.

Fey let herself sink into the chair's fabric as she drank in her view. The distance from Covista Forest kept her safe. But the more she looked at it, the more the sight of those collective trees made her mouth dry. Her throat felt scratchy as the taste rose up from the pit of her stomach. Oddly enough, it didn't taste like bile. In fact, there was no taste at all. Maybe she was getting used to it. She took another sip to make the empty taste disappear.

It's just the forest, Fey. Ferns, raccoons, trees… nothing's going to swallow you up.

She closed her eyes and shook away the growing feeling inside her. In twenty-four hours, she would be another year older. There would be another day gone by without knowing the full story. Another day when hesitation would creep up and keep her from taking a step forward.

She finished her coffee and rinsed the cup out in the sink. As she dried her hands, she looked over to the counter top where Frankie's brown bag waited. Another feeling crept up from the pit of her stomach. This time it was guilt. Fey bit her lip from the inside as she mentally swore at herself. She should probably run that to the pie shop this morning. After all, who knew how long the shelf life was on some of that stuff? She didn't want anything to end up in the garbage where another stray cat could get into it.

She slipped on her sandals and took a quick look in the mirror. Nothing of herself stood out: Pin-straight, mousy hair, a few freckles, and the tell-tale signs of tired set eyes. She pushed a few strands of hair behind her ear before grabbing the brown bag and leaving out the front door.

On her way to Pie-Pie For Now, she passed by all the familiar faces she had come to know.

"Morning, Fey!" Katrina, the head nail tech at *Spa-radic*, waved.

"Pretty day, isn't it?" Ally called out as she opened the salon doors.

"On your way to see Frankie, I see!" Claire chimed in as she waved goodbye to BettyAnne, who was holding her babysitter's hand.

"I'll tell her you said 'hi'!" Fey called back. These town pleasantries made her feel like she was being welcomed into a tight-knit kinship. Their daily repartee weaved her into their town cloth effortlessly. It was in these fleeting moments Fey felt she had moved into the Wonderland she had built up in her dreams.

But then Louise Schniber shook her from that Wonderland. "The songs have sung again. I've heard them and followed their tunes. It's the fallen! They've fallen again! And the red fox hides the bitterness under the veil of sweet."

Fey brushed off Louise's greeting just as everyone else did. She waved back, nodded her head, and continued her way to Frankie.

Fey walked into the pie shop five minutes after opening, sounding off the first chimes of the day. Frankie poked her head around the corner. "Hey there! Mornin' Buttercup!" She tied her apron around her waist and nearly skipped over to the door. "Ooh, I'm glad you finally remembered! You know, you didn't have to rush this over here so early." Frankie gave Fey a flip of her wrist and her rouge curl dropped in front of her face. "Let me get those goodies from you!" She scooped the bag from Fey's hands and set it down on a nearby table.

Fey's guilt ate her up, having waited so long to bring it by. "Sorry it took me so long. I should have brought it by right away like you asked."

Without looking up, Frankie told her, "You're imaginin' things. I never said you had to rush." She feverishly pulled out each

81

item inside and she listed them off out loud. "Arrowroot, coriander, ginger, allspice... muscovado, turbinado, and pearl sugars... mint and nutmeg... Did Claire forget the dehydrated orange peel again?" She grabbed the little bag that fell to the bottom. "Ah, perfect!" She shoved it into her apron and quickly held a finger up in the air. "Oh! Wait right there real quick! It's so good that I finally have all these in hand." She ran off to the back room again.

Seconds later, Frankie ran back out of the dining room, a terra cotta pot in her hand. "Take a look at this!" She nearly forced the plant in Fey's face.

Fey swallowed back the sick lump in her throat. "The Covista trap?"

"It's growing so quickly! June found him a friend, and I think it makes him pretty happy. Watch this!"

Frankie led Fey over to the front counter where a second plant sat. She placed down the pot in her hand next to it. Fey thought she saw the mouths smile.

Don't be ridiculous.

Fey's stomach felt sick again when Frankie pulled out a clear container from her apron pocket.

Another damned vial.

"You're going to love this!" Frankie pinched a squirming bug out of the vial with tweezers and fed it to one of the plant's open mouths.

Fey felt the blood drain from her face.

"Frankie... I-" But what was she going to say? That she wanted to face the forest? She couldn't even face these plants doing what came naturally to them.

Frankie flipped her hand in the air. "The great thing about sick cats? They come with an endless supply of plant food!"

As Frankie picked up the brown bag and carried it to the back room, Fey felt weak.

Plant food?

Cold sweat beaded on her forehead. "What...what do you mean?"

Frankie yelled from the back room. "Oh, that thing was

riddled with ticks. They were all over, eating it to the bones. Helps keep my plants healthy and strong!" There was a small silence. "So..." Frankie poked her head from the doorway. "Have you given that birthday of yours any more thought?"

"Actually, I kind of have..." Fey wiped her forehead with a spare hand towel Frankie left on the table.

"Good! Because I have been thinking about it, too! Whatever you want to do, I'll drive you there and bring the best birthday pie! So, what is it?"

"Well, I was thinking-"

"You know what would be fun?" Frankie brushed her hands together as she made her way back to the dining room. "A spa day! We can go to *Spa-radic* for facials and pedicures, then grab a drink over at Wine And Moan. If you're up for it, I'll even treat you to a new dress from Tell Me Wear."

"That sounds nice, but-"

"But nothin'! In fact, I'll let June close up the shop on her own today. I'll clock out early and we can go pick you out a new outfit to wear on our spa day!"

"Sure, I guess we can-"

The store bells chimed and in walked the first customer of the day. It was the plaid shirt man, holding his phone up to his ear.

Frankie's voice lowered to a mutter as her attention was drawn to him. "See what you get when you open the gates..."

Fey's confused expression must have won Frankie's attention back. Her voice grew to its peppy timbre. "Hold that thought until later. Work calls. I'll see you an hour before closing?" Frankie gave a wink and Fey swore her eyes darkened when she looked back at the stranger walking in the door.

"Sure, Frankie."

"See ya, Buttercup!" Frankie gave Fey a quick side-hug.

Back at home, Fey cracked open her dried botany book. Most of the pages were crinkled and stuck together. There were still a few she could flip through. Doing so, she found a page with a large fern photo at the top. She read:

Dryopteris wallichiana. The alpine wood fern. This evergreen fern is native to both India and China, but can thrive in non-native parts of the world. It performs best in shady, moist environments with well-drained soil. Once it's established in soil, it is drought tolerant, making it an easy plant to care for.

The alpine wood fern is a good choice for garden beds and borders. It can survive in indoor pots with enough sun and care. If you choose to care for it indoors, you will need to cut back the fronds when the plant becomes crowded. It survives best in woodland areas where it can grow to be three to five feet tall and just as wide.

She looked at Fern in the window.

So that's why it looks so big.

She grabbed a pair of scissors. If the book said it needed to be cut back to thrive, then that was what she would do.

With shaking hands, she lifted one of the fronds. Placing the scissors on the shaft, she snipped with her eyes shut. When she opened them, her heart beat normally again. Now, there was an opening for Fern's other leaves to spread out and breathe.

As she snipped another, the fronds extended themselves outward. She swore Fern was telling her, "Thank you."

"You're welcome." Her cheeks flushed when she realized she was talking out loud to the plant. A few more cuts and Fern looked fresh, happy, thankful for Fey's care.

With a handful of freshly cut fronds, Fey felt silly she had ever been nervous about caring for the plant. Her thumb wasn't black after all. With a little bit of practice, she was able to color it green.

Tossing the leaves into the trash interrupted Fey's relaxation. Watching the lid close down reminded her of the other plants—the Covista traps. It snapped down the same way the flytraps did over the fly in the car and the bugs in the shop. She felt her cheeks flush again.

Damned plant.

The wall clock sounded its chime. 4:00. Frankie would close up shop pretty soon. It was time to meet her for…

What are we meeting for?

Fey couldn't remember if Frankie had plans or wanted to make plans. But she promised herself one thing:

Ask about the forest.

She would ask for what she wanted, what she deserved. She was sure that, of all the town residents, Frankie would be the one to know the trails by heart. She seemed to know everything else in Soura Heights inside out.

"Am I late?" Fey asked. Frankie was waiting outside the pie shop, a plastic shopping bag swinging from her fingers.

"Late? Oh, no more than usual. I took the liberty of doin' the shoppin' myself!" Frankie stopped the bag in mid-swing and opened it up. "Ta-da!"

Fey looked inside. The black and white pattern sent a shock down her spine. She tried closing her eyes to figure out why.

The display window. This was the matching dress next to the polo shirt.

"A dress?"

"Oh come on, Buttercup. It's not like it's going to kill you. It's just a dress. Look." Frankie pulled the dress out of the bag and held it up to Fey's figure.

Reluctantly, Fey stepped forward, allowing Frankie to place it over her shoulders and assess its fit.

"Hm. Well, I think I got the right size. You might fill it out a little, but I think it stretches. And look! We'll finally get to see those legs of yours!"

Fey crossed one leg behind her ankle in an attempt to hide it. Even though she was wearing her t-shirt and jeans uniform, she felt like the dress in front of her made her feel exposed.

"Oh, and I can't forget this!" Frankie pulled something else from the bag—a black beaded chain with a sparkly black pendant hanging in the middle.

"A necklace?"

"Of course!" Frankie slipped it over Fey's head. The pendant landed in the middle of her collar bone. "A black dahlia. Isn't it pretty? It just dresses you up nicely!"

"I guess so." Frankie handed Fey the bag and dress, tucking her hair behind her ear.

Fey snapped herself out of the daze the gift put her in.

"Oh Frankie?"

"Yes?"

As Frankie adjusted her hair again, Fey noticed a red plaid bandanna around her ponytail.

Have I seen her wear that before?

"Um, I just-" She shifted the bag's weight to her other hand.

I know I've seen that somewhere.

"You just, what?"

"I wanted to ask-"

What the hell did I want to ask?

"Spit it out, Buttercup."

"Could we take a walk in Covista? For my birthday?"

Frankie's eyes darkly lit up. "Oh, don't you worry about your birthday, Buttercup. I've got all that figured out. Just meet me outside the shop tomorrow, ready to celebrate, got it?"

Fey reluctantly nodded. "Got it."

There was no use arguing. Frankie had a plan and that was that.

CHAPTER ELEVEN

One Year + Two Months Earlier

Click. Fey could hear the shutter as Bruce snapped a photo of her by the lake. Someone had left an Instamax camera at his work, and it sat in the lost and found for months before Bruce asked to take it home. Now, with it in hand, he was an amateur photographer, at least until he ran out of film.

Click. He took another of Fey as she crouched by the water and made little ripples with her finger in her reflection.

"You're going to run out of film if you keep taking pictures like that."

"Don't you worry, Honey Pot. I can always get more. Besides, don't you want to have pictures of us? Years down the road, we can flip through them like old people and say things like 'you remember when we did this?' and then fight over tiny details like the day of the week it was or what we had for lunch. And when we're *really* old, we can show our grandkids there was a time when we were young and without a face full of wrinkles and gray hair." He gave her a coy wink.

"Grandkids?" Fey stood up, walked over to Bruce, and pushed her gum into her cheek. She gave him a little nudge on his side. "You think we'll get that old together?"

"That old, and *older*, Honey Pot!" Bruce rubbed his thumb on the side of her cheek. "I'm going to be by your side for years and years watching these freckles sink into old lady wrinkles." He gave her *her* smile, the one that showed off his crooked tooth.

Fey poked his ribs and turned away. "Don't be so quick to turn me into an old lady," she joked.

As she walked away and started down the trail, Bruce snapped another photo. *Click.* "There's no turning you into one when I can keep you as young as you are right now forever." He waved one of his photos in the air as he ran after her. When Bruce caught up, he linked his fingers into hers.

Salt Point Park was the one place in Saint Paign where Fey felt she could breathe. While the pavilions and parking lots usually contained families, neighborhood gatherings, and young couples steaming their car windows, the walking paths were usually barren. Not too many people in Saint Paign went for nature trail walks, so when Bruce asked Fey where she wanted to go for date day, she didn't hesitate to suggest Salt Point.

"On your left!" a single runner yelled behind them. Wearing black running shorts and a yellow sports t-shirt, he was the only other person on the trail. Fey clung to Bruce's arm as they collectively moved to the right to let the runner pass.

They continued to circle the lake on their path, Fey pointing out things she didn't typically see outside of this man-created sanctum: Squirrels freely bouncing through the grass instead of dodging cars, birds flitting out their calls without interruption, plants that grew freely from the ground instead of in potted gardens on apartment front porch steps.

Those damned plants.

Shivers rolled down her spine.

Bruce kissed her and smiled. "Ready for lunch?" He looked over her shoulder to the open grassy field. "If we hurry, I think we can grab a spot before anyone else can."

Fey giggled. "Sure." There was no need for hurry. No one was going to take up the empty spot in the field. Salt Point field was theirs for the taking.

"On your left!" The runner had finished another lap, and Fey noticed he wore earbuds as he ran past.

Oblivious to everything. If we weren't in his way, he wouldn't even know we were here.

Bruce guided Fey off to the right and pointed over to the field. "Come on. Let's get lunch."

Opening his pack, Bruce pulled out a blanket. He handed it to Fey. "Sorry, Fey. This is the closest I can get you to that Soura Heights you've been writing about."

She spread the blanket on the ground. "Bruce, I already told you. None of that matters anymore. It's a frivolous story; inconsequential. The only place I need to be is with you."

Bruce handed her a brown paper bag and kissed her. "There's that brain of yours I love so much."

Fey opened the top of the bag. "What did you bring from Nonni's?"

He listed everything as he pulled it out of his bag. "Roasted red pepper and hummus sandwiches, fresh apples, some kind of fancy cheese, and two bags of chips."

Fey nodded as she checked her own brown bag, mentally checking off each item. "Mmmm." It was nice when Bruce could bring home meals from the deli. It sure beat microwaving Hot Pockets.

Within minutes, they finished off the last crumbs. The faint *thud thud thud* from the runner's feet indicated he was starting another lap. Bruce licked the salt off his fingertips and crumpled his trash. With his freshly cleaned fingers, he blindly reached into his backpack. "I almost forgot!" He pulled out a hardback book, navy blue with lacy gold accents printed on the cover.

Eyes widened, Fey brushed off her fingers and eagerly held out her hands. She knew exactly what it was and couldn't hold in her excitement. She rubbed her hand over the leather cover. The gold print felt smooth and raised, as if she were reading the most elusive Braille. Her heart's beat quickened its pace.

"Do you know what this is?" Fey's mouth was open in awe.

"I know it cost me a pretty penny, but it was worth every bit for that look on your face!"

"Bruce... this is..."

"One of the managers at work likes to read a lot. She's the brainy-type, real smart, like you, Fey. She brought this book in a few times to read during her lunch break. She said this was one of her favorites. When I asked her about it, she told me where she bought hers and said the book store might have another if I was interested. It was some vintage book shop downtown that smelled like cat dander and dust. I had no idea a store could hold so many... *old* books." He scratched the back of his neck. "Did you know some of those books sell for thousands?"

Fey's eyes grew wider, like a deer in the headlights.

"Oh, don't worry! It wasn't *that* much!" Bruce nervously chuckled. "Do you like it?"

Words escaped her. How he could find a first edition Emily Dickinson collection was beyond her. "You shouldn't have."

"Oh yes I should have." Bruce winked as he collected their brown bags and sandwich wrappers to find a trash can. Behind him, Fey was left laying on her stomach, propped by her elbows, exploring the pages in her new book. She couldn't believe Bruce had taken time out of his day to track down an item specifically for her, something he would have no interest in flipping through himself, but something she would devour every word as if it were butterscotch—slow and savoring.

A first edition.

The butterflies in Fey's stomach fluttered like crazy. There weren't many things she liked to put important emphasis on, but this was a thing that felt special. She didn't know where to begin to thank him for such a gift. She looked up from her spot on the ground to mutter a weak, "thanks" and found two sets of feet. One belonged to her husband. The other pair were attached to legs in black running shorts.

"Hi?" was all she could manage.

"Just click this button, here." Bruce handed the runner his Instax camera and pointed to the side shutter button. Then he ran to Fey, who was still looking up, confused from her position on the ground. Plopping next to her, Bruce placed his arm around her side, balancing his weight with his palm on the ground. Half sitting, half laying down, he posed. "CHEESE!"

Fey looked up at him in shock. Laughter escaped her as she was trying to process what was happening. Bruce must have interrupted the runner, preventing him from continuing yet another lap around the lake.

Click. Just like that, the photo was taken and the little square print slowly creeped out of the top camera slot. "Here." The runner pushed the camera forward with his sweaty hands. "I... don't want...

to touch... it.... It....would...ruin... it," he labored between breaths.

"Thank you!" Bruce hopped up from his position and took it from him. The runner nodded his head and jogged back to the trail. The *thud thud thud* of his feet faded to a distant sound.

"What was that for?" Fey asked. Her book was still open to a random page in front of her.

"I told you. For when we're old and gray. I want at least one good photo of us now. Then, we can pull it out in 60 years and remember when a sweaty stranger came over to take the picture!"

Fey laughed. "You mean we can remember how you dragged a stranger away from his exercise?"

"Same difference." Bruce showed her the photo. In it, he was half-sitting, half-laying on top of her as his smile showed off every tooth in his mouth, including the one crooked one. In the photo, she looked up at him with a smile as wide as her open book.

Bruce took the photo from her hands and pulled out his monogrammed wallet. "Well, that was the last of the film. Good thing we got a good one out of it." The leather billfold opened to two pockets. On the right, Bruce kept credit cards, Nonni's employee discount card, and any gift cards he may have collected over the years. The left side was currently empty. He filled the space with the photo. "So I can see us every time I open up my wallet."

Just then, a small feather as long as Fey's thumb drifted from the sky and gently landed on the open page of her book. She lifted it from its quill and twirled it between her fingers. She chuckled to herself as she compared it to her scar. Here, between her fingers, was a real feather, straight from a healthy, happy bird. It was nothing like the hardened skin on her arm. The shaft bisected into two colors. One side was a light blue, the shade of sky on a clear spring morning. The other side was gray, like the threads of moonlight at dusk. When she twirled it between her fingers, the two colors married together as if time itself was a blurred concept. Morning, dusk, and everything in between blended together with aplomb. With her other hand, she thumbed the lines on the page in front of her. "Hope is the thing with feathers that perches in the soul - and sings the tunes without the words - and never stops at all."

"Huh?" Bruce looked confused. "What was that?"

"Emily Dickinson." Fey pointed to her book, then held up the feather. "This feather found its way right where I was reading."

Bruce's eyes beamed. "It's a sign from the skies!"

Of course Bruce would think so.

"May I?" Bruce held his hand out, asking for the feather. He took it and twirled it around his fingers. "It's a pretty one, isn't it? I wonder what kind of bird it came from." He looked toward the sky, as if he would find the answer calling back to him. When there was no answer, Bruce flicked the tip of the feather with his finger. "Oh well, it is pretty. What was it you said? Hope is a feather?"

"The thing with feathers that perches in the soul."

"Wow. No wonder you like her so much. Sounds like Emily Dickinson really knows her stuff." He opened his wallet. "Would you mind?"

Fey shrugged her shoulders. Bruce moved the Instax photo toward the front of the pocket and tucked the feather behind it. "There. It'll live there. And if ever you're feeling sad or down or whatever, I can pull it out and remind you of that book you like so much. And of hope; it'll remind you to have hope." He tapped her gently on the head and gave her a wink.

Fey shrugged again. If Bruce wanted to keep a feather in his wallet, that was fine by her. She didn't need a token to remind her of what she loved — books, Bruce, and the real connection between them. She rubbed her arm. Her scar was token enough. And she didn't need it to remind her of hope. She had Bruce to do that enough for both of them.

CHAPTER TWELVE

Present Day

Fey stood at her front doorstep with her shopping bag in hand, gazing past her roof and at the forest treetops. Usually, the distance made her feel moderately safe, like dangling on the edge of a cliff while wearing a harness to pull her back the moment she needed. Today felt different. It felt like that harness wasn't attached to anything solid anymore. Its buckles had been loosened and she could step off that ledge at any moment and drop into the forest. A stale scent drifted through the air, and she wondered what might have made it.

The weight of her new dress and necklace tugged at her fingers from its plastic handles. Its weight grounded enough to remind her where she was—safe at home. She gripped the bag tighter with her fingertips, but Fey's mind wasn't on her new clothes. It was on what lay beyond those trees.

Stay out of the forest.

Enough is enough, Fey. Be strong. Face it. Face the forest, the trail, the trees, the...spot.

Her head spun in all directions as the records in her head skipped back and forth. She couldn't land on a single track to keep herself steady. It all felt dizzying, even as she tried to focus and tune out the things that didn't matter. The gravel behind her crunched as a car drove up her driveway. It jerked her out of her thoughts and made her jump in surprise.

Who could that be?

Tom Brickshaw's white Ford Bronco pulled into her driveway. It rolled to a stop a few feet away from her. He rolled down his window and waved. "Heya, Fey!"

She made her way over to the driver's window to greet him. "Hi, Tom. What's up?"

"Oh, I'm just on another call from good 'ol Louise down the street." He pointed out the window.

93

Fey glanced down Rosecourt Road. It was a long way from the rundown apartments where she and Bruce used to live. She could see her neighbor's house in the distance. No one had to worry about sharing walls and hearing neighbors' footsteps from the ceiling. If you wanted to interact with your neighbors, you had to make an effort.

They've fallen again. That's what she said earlier today, isn't it?

Most of the time, she made as much sense as alphabet soup, spilling out nonsense letters as she spoke with a paranoid, wide-eyed expression. Once in a while, she would call Tom out and loosely explain something that spooked her. And in perfect Tom fashion, he would show up and put his good nature to use.

"What's it this time, Tom?"

"You know how it is. It's hard to understand what she's getting at, but once in a while, she's got a lucid thought in there. Apparently, Louise found a wet footprint on her doorstep." He sighed and shrugged his shoulders. "She's convinced someone is on her property watching her or something. At least, that's what I think she said. I promised I'd come out to take a look and ask around." Tom drummed his fingers on the steering wheel. "So, before I get over there, have you seen anything suspicious? Any creepers in the bushes? Unknown cars patrolling the road? Perhaps Bigfoot walking on doorsteps?" He chuckled at his own joke.

Fey ran her mind over her walk home. She saw the same people she saw every day, Frankie, June, Claire, Katrina, Louise, and all the men and women who typically do their walking and shopping off of Busy Street. The same smiles, same waves, and same mild-mannered gestures. There weren't any cars she didn't recognize. No one was creeping around through front yards. Bigfoot didn't make an appearance. There was nothing that stood out to her as abnormal or suspicious.

"Nothing I can think of. It seems like the same old Soura Heights to me."

Tom smiled back at her. "That's okay, Fey. I figured as much. But I'm a man of my word. If I say I'm going to ask around, I'm going to. Chances are, the footprint is Louise's herself. Poor woman has probably scared herself silly. I wish she had some family around, someone to check up on her more often, you know?"

Fey nodded her head and gazed back over at the treetops. Her nose picked up the stale scent again. It was still there, leaving a taste in Fey's mouth like rancid milk.

What is that smell? It's awful.

Another breath in and the scent intensified in the breeze. It was more noxious now, pungently nauseating. More than likely, it hitched a ride in the air from some standing water or a dead animal nearby. A flattened raccoon could easily have been left behind a few feet down Rosecourt.

Raccoons. Forest.

Tom stuck his head out the driver's side window a little further.

"You alright there, Fey? You're looking a little daydreamy."

"Oh, just thinking."

"About the forest?"

"Maybe."

Stay out of the forest, Fey.

Tom looked solemnly at Fey. "It's almost the anniversary, isn't it?"

Apple pie. Polo shirt. Red splotches.

She gave Tom a small smile. "Almost a year."

Tom turned the ignition off in his car, but stayed in the driver's seat. "Fey, I know you miss him. It's good to miss him. Just don't force yourself to be over it. And don't mull over the whys and what ifs. It'll only drive you crazy. It's not worth it. The forest eats out-of-towners up all the time. It's no one's fault. One step off the trail and it's the wrong one. There's no one to blame, not even the person taking that step."

Fey looked down at her feet. Her eyes stung and her vision blurred. Her mouth felt dry and wet at the same time, like she ate something that didn't fully agree with her. Swallowing it down, she blinked her eyes clear. She knew he was right. She wasn't looking for anyone to blame. She was only looking to be the strong woman she wanted to be. The strong woman Frankie saw her as.

95

Be strong. You are strong.

"I know, Tom."

Tom uneasily shifted his weight in his seat. "Say," he pointed to the bag she held. "Is there a sale over at Tell Me Wear? The wife's been wanting to go shopping again. I told her to wait until the prices go down. The clothes she comes home with from there are always a pretty penny and they don't pay me a nickel more than they need to for me to wear this fancy shirt." He pointed to his uniform. "I can't afford for her to refill her closet every few weeks, you know."

Fey jiggled the bag in her hand. "Tell Peggy I'm sorry. There's no sale. Just a birthday gift thanks to Frankie."

Tom started the Bronco back up and put both hands on the wheel. "Good 'ol Frankie, always looking out for everyone and doing her best to keep us all happy here. She's what keeps our little community together, isn't she? I don't know what we'd do without our little pie maker. I'll have to tell Peggy to wait another week until the sale racks fill up." He gave Fey a half-smile. "Now, off to do my duty. I need to go check out that mysterious footprint of Louise's before it dries up. As always, give me a ring if you see anything suspicious in the area."

"Sure will."

"And happy birthday!"

"Not for a few days, Sheriff."

"Close enough. Happy birthday, anyway."

Tom backed out of Fey's driveway. She watched as his Bronco disappeared down the road. Poor Louise was probably pacing her living room, waiting for Tom to arrive as the wet footprint on her doorstep slowly disappeared. No doubt, an evaporating footprint would make the crazy in her amplify even more. And poor Tom was going to spend the rest of the evening trying to decode Louise's ramblings.

Fey shook her head to clear it. She looked back out at those trees and took a deep breath. She wondered how Louise became the endearing 'town crazy'. When did the crazy start? When did she lose all sense of meaning? When did the paranoia kick in? Was it quick, right after she lost her husband? Or did it slowly unravel itself after years of isolation?

She closed her eyes and took a second, deeper breath.

Maybe it started out just like this, mulling over the past, creating a new future, and blending the two until you don't know up from down. Before you know it, you're calling the cops about your own wet footprint on your doorstep.

Fey shook herself free of her thoughts. If she was going to fall into Louise's footsteps and fill in her place as another town crazy, then there was nothing that would stop her.

When she stepped inside, she threw her shopping bag on the floor in the corner. It sat there looming over her like fabric in the shadows. Thinking about slipping into it for longer than a few minutes made her feel uncomfortable, like putting it on would be inviting an inevitable disaster.

Fey took a seat by the big living room window and wondered about what was behind all those trees. Crazy isn't dressing in mismatched clothes filled with holes and stains. Crazy isn't talking in circles wide eyed to anyone with two ears. Crazy isn't losing a spouse and learning how life is supposed to be lived without them. It's not uprooting yourself to start in a town that is seemingly perfect by imagination alone. It's not the fear of a wet footprint by your front door or calling out random expressions no one around you will ever understand themselves.

Crazy was pushing out the voice of reason when it's what has driven you to stay safe for years. Crazy was dropping what you know as fact to face the 'what ifs' and 'hows' and 'whys'. Crazy was the desire to come face to face with the woods that claimed your husband almost a year ago. Crazy was deciding to find the exact place he died to see how accidental the accident really was.

Stay out of the forest.

The smell from earlier lingered in her nose and she wondered what the source really was. Sure, rotting raccoons were common, but this wasn't a smell that typically wafted past her house. If it did come from something squashed from car tires, surely the scent would have been more familiar. No, this smelled like it came from something other than roadkill. She was sure the smell came from something bigger. Much bigger.

CHAPTER THIRTEEN

One Year + One Month Earlier

Bruce set his keys and grocery bag on the dining table when he came home from work. "Hey, Honey Pot! How was your day?"

Fey looked up from the couch where she had settled in with a book. Bruce's mouth broke into an impish grin. "Good... what's up with that look?"

"I finally did it, Fey!"

"Did what?"

"I'm moving up!"

Fey lay her book in her lap. "What do you mean?"

"Fey, they're going to make me a manager!"

"Who is? Nonni's?"

"They're sending me to a training conference next month!" Bruce ran over her to her, and his excited arms scooped her off the couch. He pressed himself into her, nuzzling her neck. His day-old facial hair lightly scratched her cheek.

"We should celebrate!"

"Celebrate? But, Bruce, you sure this is the job you want? Grocery store manager?"

Bruce was already by the counter, pulling out a pie from the grocery bag.

"Honey Pot, of course this isn't my dream job. But it's a step up, isn't it? It'll be more hours and I might need to take a few weekends for training here and there, but the pay is better and I'll finally get us some good benefits."

Bruce pulled his hand out of the grocery bag again. This time, he held a block of cheese. He wiggled it in the air, over the pie.

"Plus, a little more time at Nonni's as manager, and I'll have the experience to get a better job elsewhere. Maybe we could afford to move to that town you love so much—Soura...?"

Fey shook her head. "Bruce, I told you, that's unnecessary.

Home is with you." With that, Fey wrapped her arms around him, breathing in his scent. He smelled like freshly baked bread. "So… pie, huh? With cheese?"

Bruce squeezed her back.

"You'd be surprised how good they are together. The current manager had some in the break room earlier as a celebration before she left her job. I still can't believe I'm going to take her place. Apparently, it's some kind of tradition from France or something. At least that's what the other cashier, Sean, said. I think you may like it."

Bruce kissed her on the top of her head. "Of course you'd know that." He slunk away from her arms to bring the pie and cheese into the kitchen where he fixed two plates.

Fey peered at the bookcase across the room. One of those dusty cookbooks was bound to have a dessert section.

One day, I'll bake our own apple pie.

The microwave beeped and Bruce brought Fey's plate out to her with a fork. Melted cheese dripped off the side of a poorly cut slice. She accepted the fork and stabbed the pie with it. She blew away the steam from the oozing cheese and took a bite with her eyes closed. The flavors worked surprisingly well together. She opened her eyes and nodded an approval.

"See? I knew you'd like it." Bruce winked at her.

Fey smiled in his direction and took another bite off her plate.

This does make for a nice celebration pie.

When they found the pie pan cleared in front of them, Fey and Bruce rubbed their full bellies with delight.

"Well, I guess that's that, huh?"

"Do we order dinner?"

"I think we just ate our dinner."

Fey nodded in agreement. As she gathered and cleaned the dishes in the kitchen, Fey heard Bruce turn on the T.V. There was a faint *click* and she knew he was choosing something to watch from his Chuck Norris DVD collection.

As she dried the last dish, she listened for the familiar dialogue, trying to place which movie he chose. It was hard to hear over the upstairs neighborhood's footsteps. They must have just gotten home, clearly making rounds in every corner of their apartment.

She leaned against the sink, trying to hear past the muffled noise. As she did, she bumped Fern. Startled at the swinging planter, she held out her hands to stop it from falling off the hook. Relief rushed through her when she realized it was safe, only to see some of the leaves sway in her direction. They brushed against each other, making a repetitive *tsk tsk tsk.*

"Sorry, Fern." Fey flushed, embarrassed for speaking out loud to a plant.

In the living room, Fey found Bruce watching *Forest Warrior.* *So that's what he chose.*

She shuddered as the screen panned across tall evergreens and Chuck Norris fought off a group of loggers. Owls and raccoons watched from overhead and Bruce was on the couch, karate-chopping in the air. No matter how much he enjoyed it, all Fey could think about was Billy and death.

To occupy her mind, she grabbed her Moleskine notebook. Over the past few months, she filled it with details of what Soura might feel like. Running her hand over her own handwriting, she wondered how serious Bruce might have been.

"Hey Bruce?"

"Hmm?" Another air chop.

"Do you really think we could go to Soura sometime?"

"Hmm?"

"I mean, we wouldn't have to transplant ourselves there. Just, take a look around. See if it might be worth it in the future. You know, if that's what you wanted?"

Bruce didn't respond. He was too absorbed in the T.V.

She ran her hands over the pages again. It was silly, really, to wonder how much the real Soura Heights would match up to her fictional image. But then again, it wasn't impossible, was it? To believe there could be a small town full of people wanting to ditch the T.V.s and computers and telephones and focus on real people.

CHAPTER FOURTEEN

Present Day

Fey pulled a chicken pot pie out of the oven and breathed in the savory aroma. Comparing it to the photo in the cookbook, it was a train wreck. Goo leaked from the sides and the crust flaked off in burnt patches. But still, it was better than the microwave and she still hadn't burned down her house.

Fey sat down at the table in the same seat she always sat in. She looked over at the chair next to her, Bruce's chair. The leg had been mended with wood glue after it broke the day they spilled out of the chair, the same day Bruce had fallen and hit his head.

Fallen. They've fallen again.

She could still see the solidified droplet from when Bruce accidentally overapplied the adhesive. Fey could have replaced the broken chair when she moved, but she wasn't ready to let go of the memories associated with it. She wasn't ready to put them behind her. At the first bite of her meal, she heard a knock at the door.

Who could that be?

She couldn't imagine anyone paying her a visit now. Interrupting a person's meal wasn't part of Soura's vernacular. Cautiously, she walked to the front door and looked through the peephole. For the second time in 48 hours, Tom Brickshaw was on Fey's property. This time, he stood on her front porch, dressed completely in his uniform.

Fey opened the door, eyebrows raised. "Everything okay, Tom?"

Tom took his hat off. "Mind if I come in, Fey?"

The tone in his voice was dolefully familiar. He wasn't stopping in for a chat about clothing sales for Peggy, she was sure of that. She stepped aside and offered the sofa to him. "Come on in."

Tom gingerly stepped in and took his hat off. He opened his mouth to talk, but stopped himself as he saw the full plate of food on the table. "Oh, I'm so sorry. Am I interrupting?"

"Not at all." Fey sat down at her chair. "Do you mind if I finish this?"

Tom shook his head. "I suppose not." He twiddled his thumbs in silence as Fey took a few more bites of the meal she could no longer fully enjoy with him sitting there.

Across the room, Tom rubbed his knuckles and scratched the top of his head. He drummed his thumbs on his lap and massaged the back of his neck. It was as if he had a thousand little tics to occupy himself without saying a word. It was like he was two people: one who confidently walked in, ready to speak with authoritative clarity, and one who was nervously waiting for the right time to start.

Apple pie.

Fey closed her eyes and tried to clear a dizzy spell she felt creeping up. She quickly shoved the rest of her food into her mouth and ate. She resented Tom for rushing her meal, but when she was done, she took a seat next to him. Heart racing, she nodded to cue him that she was ready.

Tom sighed. "Say, Fey. Do you know who Richard Teft is?"

Fey's eyebrows furrowed. That was not what she expected. She shook her head. "No." For a moment, she was relieved to hear a name she didn't recognize.

Who the hell is Richard Teft? What does he have to do with me?

Tom furrowed his eyebrows, too. "I didn't think so, but I needed to ask. Are you sure you haven't seen or heard anything unusual?"

Fey shook her head again. What on earth was Tom getting at? She may have only lived here for a year, but it was long enough to get to know almost everyone in town. There wasn't a single face she couldn't name nor a face she couldn't picture. That is, except for Richard Teft. There was no one in Soura Heights by that name, she was sure of it.

Tom's hands clapped in a soft *thud* as if he was giving his stamp of approval. "Well, that's good." He shuffled his feet once more as he paused. "Listen, Fey. Something happened I think you should know. Given your...circumstances, I think I need to tell you."

"So, are you going to disclose why you're here, Tom?" Fey was eager for him to spit it out.

He rubbed his hands together nervously. "I went to see our friend, Louise, like I said. You know, to check on her and all."

"Did something happen? Is Louise okay?" At the sound of a familiar name, Fey's worry made her voice waver.

"No, no." Tom shook his head. "Louise is fine. Like I said, I paid her a visit. She showed me the footprint, which was barely there anymore, but I did take a look at it. It didn't seem too threatening in itself, but I promised her I'd look around for anyone or anything that might have left it. I looked around her property, in the bushes and the overgrown weeds, but couldn't find anything else suspicious."

Why isn't he getting to the point?

"So... the footprint?"

"It was nothing, nothing at all. In fact, I compared it to her muddy shoe and it pretty much matched up perfectly in shape and size. I'm pretty sure the print was hers. And I did my best to assure her there was nothing to worry about. But I didn't come here to tell you about a footprint that leads to nothing."

"Okay."

So why the hell are you here?

"You know how she is. She likes to talk, and she talked a lot. And I did my best to listen. Something about birds singing and other animals talking? Whistling? Dancing? Maybe it was people dancing? I don't know. I really don't know what she was getting at. But, I listened. When she was done, there was nothing else I could do for her. I told her I was sorry I couldn't help and gave her my card if she needed to call again. She got real quiet and her eyes got big like they do sometimes. I figured she was done. But when I opened her front door, she did something she's never done before. She grabbed my arm, tight."

Tom reached out and grabbed Fey by the arm to demonstrate. It felt like the day Bruce grabbed her arm at the dining table, the same day he had fallen. She could feel his fingers dig into her skin, sure to leave bruise marks later. "Like this. She pulled my arm toward her and leaned in so close I could see the pores in her skin. She said, 'They've fallen again, Sheriff. The leaves have crunched and the day stars flew over. They've fallen, they've fallen, and the sky cries out gray and brown!' Or... it was something like that. And then she pointed over to Covista." He shrugged his shoulders and pointed out her window.

Fey shifted in her seat to shake Tom's grip.

They've fallen. Isn't that what Louise said the other day, too? What did she mean?

Tom apologetically moved his hand away. "Sorry, Fey. I didn't mean to startle you. I don't know what day stars are or what she meant about the sky turning colors, but it seemed like she wanted me to check out Covista Forest." He shrugged again. "You know me, Fey. I work to protect this community of ours. It's my whole purpose here. I don't want anyone hurt and I don't want anyone unsafe. I'm a man of my word. If someone needs me to check something out, I'm going to check it out. That includes Louise, even if I don't understand her, even if she's crazy."

Tom rubbed the back of his neck. Fey thought she could see sweat form on his forehead. "So, I drove out to Covista and parked by the main trail. I figured even if Louise was barking off nonsense, at least I'd get some exercise in. I started at the main trail and followed it. A little over a fourth a mile in, I heard some animals growling. Well, not really growling, but definitely making noise."

Fey sat with her eyes fixed on him as he told his story.

Apple pie.

"I shined my light through the trees off the trail to see what was going on. At first, it didn't seem like anything, just a couple of foxes fighting over something to eat. A dead bird, a mouse, something like that. I was going to brush it off and head on back to the station, but there was this nagging feeling telling me I needed to look into it further." He paused.

"So, what did you do?" Fey was trying to follow his story. She didn't understand why he was walking her through the details instead of cutting to the chase. Regardless, her mouth had turned dry in anticipation.

"I stepped a little closer, which spooked the foxes pretty quickly. That nagging feeling kept telling me I needed to search for whatever it was they were fighting over, so I walked into the woods a little more. I had to go a few feet in to find what it was." He rubbed his hands together a little. "Sorry, Fey, maybe I shouldn't be telling you all of this after all. I just thought maybe... maybe... maybe I should? I was hoping in some way it will help." His voice cracked a little.

"Help? Help me? How?"

Fey was having a feeling of deja vu.

White polo. Red splotches.

"Fey, those foxes were fighting over a body. A lifeless body laying on the forest floor." He must have felt Fey's eyes judging him. "Oh, don't worry, I did a little bit of an investigation on my own as I always do in these situations. See, it's happened many times before. People don't know any better and lose track of where they are out there. They fall, get hurt, and that's that. Once in a while, someone will find...pieces. Pieces with unusual bite marks. Like an animal got to them. A bear or wildcat ... or something. I suppose that's what the foxes were doing. It doesn't look like there was any foul play. No one was around. There wasn't anything that indicated a fight. It's like it always is. He just walked off the trail in the wrong direction."

Fey felt numb. "A body? How... how did that happen?"

"My guess? He probably tripped and hit his head. There are thousands of rocks and stumps and God knows what else. If you don't know where you're going, it would be easy to do. He had a head injury and his clothes were ripped, both of which could easily happen out there in the overgrown brush. It really doesn't take much. I checked his wallet. His name is Richard Teft. That's it. I don't know anything about him except that. The forest just... ate him up."

Ate. Him. Up.

"Tom, what do you mean it's like how it always is?"

Tom rubbed the back of his neck. "Oh, I don't know, Fey. Lots of people don't know what they're doing out there. I've lost count over how many times it's happened. I know it's over twenty."

Fey pictured the lifeless body laying on the forest floor, limp and torn, beaten up by the forest overgrowth, bloody from injury. His head was probably off to the side, his mouth and eyes slightly open without life breathing out of them. Was he married? Did he have children? Who were his loved ones? Would Tom Brickshaw deliver the news himself? Or would he call for someone else to do the dirty work for him? Fey swallowed away the unease growing inside her throat.

"What...What was he wearing?"

"Wearing? Oh... I guess it was a plaid button-up shirt and jeans." Tom looked confused. "Why, Fey? Do you think you might know who he is? Do you know something?"

Fey shook her head. No, she didn't know Richard Teft. She had never heard the name before now. But the clothing description was eerily familiar. All week, she had seen a red plaid shirt. He had been in Pie-Pie For Now. He had walked the cobblestone street. He had leaned against the walls of A Pair of Dice Lost. He had come and gone in and out of Fey's peripheral.

The man she had wondered about all week long was Richard Teft.

And now, Richard Teft had fallen, just as Louise said. Fallen, just like Bruce.

CHAPTER FIFTEEN

One Year Earlier

At 6:30AM, Fey woke up to the buzz of Bruce's alarm clock. From the nightstand, it sounded off its morning call loud enough to jolt anyone awake out of a peaceful sleep. Anyone, that is, except Bruce.

"Bruce. Bruce! It's time to get up." She shook his shoulder in an attempt to jostle him awake. He shook free of her hands and rolled to the side, ignoring her efforts.

She tried a little louder as the timer continued to rattle. "Bruce! Time to wake up!"

He pulled the bed sheet over his head to hide away from her voice.

Mischievously, Fey ran her hand under the bed sheet and pulled it over her head, too. Under the tent of covers, Fey could see the outline of his tousled hair. Her fingers found the bottom of his sleep shirt and pulled it up, exposing his navel and the little tuft of hair leading to his boxers.

She circled his belly button with a single finger and leaned her mouth to his ear. "It's morning. Time to get up," she whispered. Her hand began to follow the lower tuft of hair.

"Hmm...?" Bruce stretched his arms up and turned the alarm off. It was now 6:45. "Oh, morning, Honey Pot." He leaned over and kissed her on the forehead. "Guess today's the day, isn't it?"

Fey pulled her hand away and greeted Bruce with a kiss on the cheek. "It sure is."

Fifty miles away, a large hotel would greet Bruce and several other employees from Nonni's all over the area. Tomorrow, he would be Nonni's new front end manager and one step closer to a big house with a white fence off of Mercury Lane.

Fey smiled and breathed in Bruce's morning scent. His sour breath didn't bother her. It was raw and real. It made her feel grounded. It made her feel at home. She guided his arm around her waist and beckoned him to stay another minute like this.

Another kiss on the forehead. "Sorry, Honey Pot. Gotta get ready." He rolled over and climbed out of bed, dropping his sleep shirt and boxers to the floor, readying himself for the shower. "Gotta jump in quickly if I'm going to make it on time!" Fey watched him walk naked to the bathroom, her cheeks pinkening. His bare form was taut and inviting. The butterflies in her fluttered like confetti in her heart. Again, she wondered how Plain-Jane-Fey could have ever ended up with Studly-Steve-Bruce.

At 6:52, she rolled out of bed in her flowered nightgown and pulled the sheets up tight by the pillows. She smoothed down the covers to secure them in place. If Bruce was going to drive almost an hour away for training, he would need a good breakfast to wake him up. Before heading into the kitchen, she grabbed a stick of gum off the nightstand to ward off her own morning breath.

Breakfast was ready at 7:15. Fey had a plate full of microwaved bacon and toast by the time Bruce was showered and dressed. He looked handsomely clean cut in his white polo shirt and khaki pants—something he had mulled over for weeks to wear. She sat his plate in front of him and took her own place at the table.

Bruce steadied himself in his chair. The broken leg was glued back together, with a little dried wood glue glob where it dripped. He pointed to her Moleskine notebook as he shoveled bacon into his mouth. "Are you going to work on that some more today?"

"Yeah, sure," Fey answered him. She moved the notebook out of reach. She didn't want to dream about 'one day' right now. "But first, what about your training? How long will you be gone?'

Bruce shoveled more of his breakfast into his mouth. He gave her a small shrug. "I'm really not sure, Honey Pot. They said training can take a few hours, but who knows what traffic will be like coming out. I suppose I could be out all day." Fey frowned. She didn't like the idea of Bruce being away all day, especially in some hotel seemingly far away. "Expect me home for dinner, though. I wouldn't miss it for the world. Especially since we'll need to celebrate. Celebration pie?"

She gave a small smile. "I'll pick some up before you get back."

"Good. Make it an extra good one. I have a feeling we will have a little extra to celebrate tonight!" Bruce gave her a knowing wink.

"I have no idea what you're up to, Bruce Anderson, but you better finish up breakfast. I don't want you speeding there to be on time."

Fey watched her husband lick his plate clean. When he finished, she slyly added, "But if you want to accelerate on the way home, that would be okay…. You sure you don't know what time you'll be back?"

"Not an exact time, but it'll be here before you know it. After all, I wouldn't miss your birthday." Bruce gave her *her* smile. Even though it was Fey's birthday, a celebration for her wasn't on her mind. The day would still be there when he got home and she would still be 20 the next day and the day after.

Bruce brought his empty plate into the kitchen at 7:30. He gave Fern a quick drink, turned the planter in the sun, and came back to the table where Fey had her story open in front of her. Her eyes were fixed on the open page, waiting for something real to magically appear.

Bruce leaned over and gave her a little goodbye nuzzle. She felt his facial hair rub the side of her cheek and felt comfort in its slightly scratchy texture. Reaching behind her, Fey could feel Bruce's shirt collar had popped up. She reached her arms up and around his neck to fix it. She took a moment to notice the emblem on his shirt. It was a tiny golden horse jockey riding a tiny golden horse. It suited him well. She patted down his collar and smoothed it in place.

"Thanks, Honey Pot!" Bruce gave her his charming side smile, the same one that made her feel lucky all over again, with the one crooked tooth.

She blushed as those butterflies crept up on her again. "Sure."

The clock read 7:45AM.

"Look at that time! I better get going before I'm late."

"Good luck. I'll have a celebration pie waiting for you when you get home." She eyed the bookcase. If he expected an extra special celebration, she would make an extra special celebration pie.

He leaned over and gave her a quick kiss on the forehead. "I can't wait!" He opened the door a little, but turned back around before he left. "If the apartment gets too quiet while I'm gone, I've left a DVD in the player for you."

Fey gave a tiny giggle, then in unison, they gave each other a mock karate chop in the air. Bruce gave her one last kiss goodbye and walked out the door. From the driver's seat, he motioned to his mouth to alert her to her own gum chewing. She waved once more and pocketed the gum in her cheek. Fey thought about how the next time she would see her husband, he would have a new title, a new paycheck, and a new jolt of energy taking pride in his hard work.

At 7:50AM, Fey watched him pull out of the parking lot. She had watched his car pull away thousands of times before. Each time, she waited eagerly for him to fill the parking spot back up with his Jeep Wrangler so he could greet her with *her* smile and a hello nuzzle.

It'll be here before you know it.

His words rang in her ears.

Fey secured the couch corner, her Moleskine notebook on her lap. For hours, she scribbled down notes, then scribbled right through them. Nothing that came to her felt right. As much as she ached for a place that valued connections, she couldn't form a connection through her imagination any longer.

At 11:15, Fey looked out the window at Bruce's empty parking space and wished she knew when it would fill back up.

A Nonni's deli sandwich waited for her in the fridge for 11:30 lunch. Roasted red pepper hummus on rye. Bruce sure knew how to pick a good almost-expired food from the shelf.

At 11:50, she took a break to use the restroom. As she washed her hands, her reflection stared back from the mirror. She wished her freckles weren't so prominent and her hair wouldn't hang so unswervingly straight. Then, the corner of the bathroom mirror caught her eye. There, a tiny heart written in marker waited for her. Bruce's little love note to her.

At 12:00, Fey pulled a cookbook off the shelf. She flipped to the dessert section and found a recipe for apple pie.

Why the hell does the crust take so long?

If she was going to have a celebration pie done and ready before Bruce came home, she needed to get going to Nonni's now.

The parking lot was full at 1:22, and she had to park in the back between two large pickup trucks. The store bustled with people pushing carts down every aisle. Fey took a deep breath. With the aisles packed with customers, it was going to take some tricky maneuvering to get in and out in enough time.

Fey pulled her grocery list out of her pocket. The paper's edge frayed from ripping it out of her notebook. Seeing the imperfect tear, Fey regretted not searching for something else to write on. She feared she would come home to a pile of loose papers.

As she weaved through the other shoppers, Fey filled her basket. She was surprised how much a bag of honeycrisp apples weighed down her cart. She slung flour and sugar in, too. By the time she reached the dairy aisle, she wasn't sure which cheese to grab. She ended up with shredded cheddar. If the crust alone was going to take hours, she didn't want to waste her time slicing a block.

"Find everything okay, ma'am?"

She nodded quietly at the cashier, but couldn't help feeling a little lost in his words.

Ma'am?

The cashier in front of her had short blond hair. His voice spiked high at the word "okay." Without reading his nametag, she knew this was Sean. The same Sean that Bruce had mentioned to her in stories after work. The same Sean who (wrongly) told Bruce where their celebration pie came from.

In the Soura Heights she imagined, cashiers knew everyone who walked into their market regardless whether their husbands were employees or not. The Sean equivalent would greet her by name and ask if Honeycrisp apples made better pie than gala. He'd offer her tips to getting the temperature just right and share the secrets of his own recipe. Then, he would tell her to have a great day and to pass their well wishes to Bruce.

She brushed off Sean's greeting, paid for her things, and climbed back in her car with groceries in tow. The time on her dash read 2:50.

Maybe he made it home early.

Fey spent her drive home imagining the look on Bruce's face when he welcomed her home. She imagined his description of the free meal they provided and how it compared to Nonni's deli. She imagined him slumped in the corner of the couch, exhausted from the drive and ready for a microwaved meal, celebration pie, and a Chuck Norris marathon until they fell asleep.

The jeep's parking spot was still empty at 3:12.

Fey dropped her bags on the table, knocking her notebook from the place she left it. She had been right. Ripping out a page tore the binding loose. A few scribbled pages were already falling away from the cover.

At 3:30, Fey found herself fighting over the dough. She added water when it felt too dry. Then, it stuck to her fingers so much she had to add more flour. It yo-yoed between too sticky to touch and too dry to mould for several attempts before she finally gave up and decided it was good enough at 4:10.

Whoever would choose to make pies for a living must be a special kind of masochist.

By 4:15, she had the dough wrapped in the fridge and Chuck Norris filled in the background as she waited for the next step. She imagined Bruce walking through the front door, excited to see her making use of the DVD he left. She imagined him nuzzling her and surprised at the bag of apples waiting on the table. She attempted to mend her notebook while she waited.

At 6:00, the movie ended. Fey gave up on the notebook and prepared herself for another battle round. Filling the crust proved to be easier than making it. By 6:25, it was in the oven.

She pictured Bruce opening the front door to the welcoming cinnamon scent that filled their tiny home. She pictured him walking into the living room with arms open and bags under his eyes. She pictured him tired and ready to make a meal of celebration pie and Chuck Norris.

The pie timer finally went off at 7:23PM. As the pie cooled on the stove, Fey looked out the window at the darkening sky. Bruce's parking space was still empty. A small blue and gray bird landed on a

113

branch in view. It shook its feathers and reminded Fey of the feather Bruce kept in his wallet—his hope feather.

She pictured Bruce drumming his fingers on the steering wheel in traffic. She thought about him making a pit stop by Nonni's on the way home. She pictured him debating between two ice creams and deciding to bring both home because the celebration needed to be that big. She pictured him opening the front door, ready to collapse within the cushions of the couch.

Fey's stomach grumbled. At 7:32, a microwaved meal was hot enough to eat.

By 8:14P.M., She cleaned up her empty plate and checked on Fern. The soil was still wet from this morning. She turned the planter just in case it needed it. One of the feathered fronds touched her and sent chills down her spine.

She covered the pie at 8:20 and placed it in the fridge. It wouldn't be a celebration pie if she ate it alone. By herself, it would just be apple pie and cheese.

At 9:00, Fey worked on her notebook again. Just when she thought she had the paper secure, the binding broke for the second time. All the pages fluttered to the floor. With blurry eyes, she scooped them up and piled them together. Only now, nothing was in order. Nothing made sense.

Damn it.

Angry at wasted energy, she threw the lot in the trash. It didn't matter anymore. Soura was as good as nonexistent anyway. She was bound to a life in Saint Paign.

At 10:00, she dried her eyes. She heard the neighbors walking in circles through the ceiling and cursed at them.

It was 10:42PM. Fey took one last look out the window at Bruce's empty parking space and hoped she would see his headlights shine through the window soon. She yawned at the moonlit sky and sank into the grooves in their living room sofa.

She imagined him sneaking in the front door and finding her asleep. She imagined him crawling onto the couch and curling his body to fit the grooves of hers, whispering "Happy birthday" in her ear. She imagined him disregarding dinner, celebration pie, and any possible ice cream to fall asleep next to her. She imagined waking up in the morning to the familiar sounds of his breathing, just like she did every morning.

He'll be here before I know it.

She fell asleep on the couch, alone, at 11:59, a minute before her birthday ended.

CHAPTER SIXTEEN

Present Day

After Tom left her home, Fey sat in unrest. He left her with a pitiful wave goodbye. He didn't even offer an "I'm sorry" for re-traumatizing her.

She wished Bruce were with her. She wished she could pop in one of those god-awful Chuck Norris DVDs and waste the night away with fake air karate chops while under the cover of blankets.

She visited Fern in the kitchen. As she turned the planter, she realized how happy it looked with the fresh trim. It seemed like not long ago Bruce had brought home the scrawny plant. Now, it was thriving in the little pot it lived in. It looked like its own miniature forest, like it belonged out there within the brush under the oak and sycamore trees.

To protect Richard Teft.

Why would Richard Teft end up a meal for scavengers off the forest trails? Tom said it was one of those things that happened; that the forest just "eats them up". But this was the first time Fey actually heard of it happening. At least the first time since her move.

They've fallen. They've fallen again.

Fey looked at the clock. 8:30 P.M. There was a chance Louise was still awake. Fey grabbed a sweater and slipped on her sandals. She needed to know what Louise knew.

Grass blades tickled her toes through the sandals. Her feet felt wet with the leftover rainwater from the storm. She remembered the cat calling out before the sky opened up and poured down on her and the rest of Soura Heights. She again wondered if the cat was Patches calling for help.

Within a few minutes, she was at Louise's front door. The house light was on, lightly illuminating the dingy windows. The house was in the same ranch style as Fey's, but showed more age. A piece of siding sagged by the front window and the paint on the door crackled into a pattern from the baking sun. The front porch creaked under her feet and Fey noticed the faint signs of muddy footprints as she stepped up to the front door.

Maybe she wasn't making up the footprints after all.

Fey tentatively knocked on the glass pane, hoping the old lady wasn't already asleep. What would Louise say if she answered? What would she say to Louise?

After a minute of waiting, Fey knocked a few taps again, slightly louder. She waited, listening for any movement from inside. She was about to try for a third time when she saw the doorknob jiggle. She stepped backward to give some breathing room between herself and the door.

The door cracked open and light trickled out. Fey could see Louise's round eyes peeking through the little space between the door and its frame. They widened further when they landed on Fey, adding even more wrinkles than usual to Louise's forehead. Fey could hear her whisper, but couldn't make out anything she said.

"Good evening, Louise. I'm sorry, I know it's late. I was just wondering… did you talk to Sheriff Brickshaw yesterday?"

Louise's eyes darted from side to side. Then, she cracked the door open slightly more. "It's the lynx with the kitty cat curiosity in its little yellow eyes."

Fey squinted her eyes as the door squeaked open enough for her to see Louise's whole self. She was dressed in what Fey assumed was nightwear. Only, her drawstring shorts were missing a string. Louise's frail frame was nearly lost within her oversized clothes. Her feet were bare and noticeably dirty, caked with dried mud. Had Tom noticed the condition of Louise's feet, he wouldn't have needed to compare the footprint to her shoes.

"I'm sorry, Louise. Is it a bad time?"

Louise left the door open and quietly sat on her couch, facing it. Fey took that as an invitation to join her. The yellow-brown flowered pattern was reminiscent of the 1970s. One armrest had a large tear in the fabric and the middle cushion was completely missing. Fey took in the rest of her surroundings as she sunk into the lifeless couch. Dusty shelves with broken trinkets hung uneven on the walls. There were open magazines with pages torn out and scattered on the floor. Through the signs of depravity, Fey felt this house was as lonely as Louise. Both were in need of care and attention from loving hands.

For the first time, Fey took in the deep wrinkles of Louise's hands. What had she gone through to be here, alone as her life falls apart in a house falling apart around her? Her heart ached for the lady in front of her, not yet a shell, but not quite whole anymore either.

Why the hell am I here again?

"The white star birds never lie."

Fey looked at Louise in surprise. "The white star birds?"

"The white star birds. They called their truth song. I heard it. I heard their song. It doesn't lie. They never do. Their songs are coated in truth telling even when no one wants to hear." Louise turned to Fey, her sunken eyes both sad and scared, somehow both wide and drooping at the same time. "Has the lynx heard it? Does she know their truth song? Have you looked to the day stars and *really* listened to their music?"

Fey shook her head.

Louise dropped her head back behind her and, panic stricken, stared at the ceiling. "The lynx ears aren't ready to listen yet. It's the sound of broken findings and necessity. And they don't lie. And they sing it in circles around and around and around until your head is dizzy and confused." Louise grabbed her head as she talked, moving it around and around in wide circles.

Fey felt dizzy and confused herself. She had never heard of white star birds and didn't know anything about their songs.

Searching for something to focus on, Fey noticed a small round table in front of her. It had three legs and leaned where one was a little crooked. It was as if the bottom of the leg had snapped off long ago and had been roughly glued back together. It reminded her of Bruce's chair at home and she wondered what story it held within its repair.

A framed photograph sat on top of the table with a large crack in the glass. Out of all the items displayed and scattered about Louise's home, this one seemed significant—purposefully displayed where Louise could easily view it from her position on the couch. Fey gingerly picked it up and rubbed away some of the dust with her thumb. Even though the cracked glass distorted the image, she could make out two faces. One was a young man in his twenties, wearing suspenders and a dress shirt. Through his bushy mustache, a proud smile beamed at the young lady on his arm. Her billowy peasant top fell across her shoulders and she wore her iron-straightened hair parted down the middle and behind one ear. There was no mistaking those wide set eyes. This was Louise. The man next to her must have been her husband. Though the photo's color had faded over time, Fey could still feel the amount of life captured in it. It reminded Fey of the photo Bruce captured at the park years ago and kept in his wallet. There was a story within this frame, waiting to be told.

Fey thought back to her life with Bruce, how she used to hang on his arm, hold him close, and soak up the tiny minutiae in his mannerisms. That was a time when life was abundant with carefree evenings and shared microwavable meals. It was a time with picnics in the park and jaunts down Mercury Lane. It was a time when it didn't matter where she was as long as she could lean on Bruce and feel the scruff on his chin as he nuzzled her neck. That seemed like another lifetime ago. She was glad Louise had felt that way once before, too, and wondered if the time between then and now felt even longer to Louise.

"Is this your husband? I don't think I have ever seen a picture of him before."

Louise hung her head. Her eyes saddened. "The white star birds sang for him, too. They sang in circles over and over and over again and again and again. I heard their song and followed its notes. I danced to their tune in circles, but I didn't get dizzy. Not right away. Not until the Todds and Vixens talked over them. Their voices can be louder than the white stars. That's when they made my head feel dizzy and fuzzy and dazey and hazy." Louise closed her eyes tightly and swallowed hard. Then, she opened them back up and looked at Fey directly. "They like to do that, you know? They like it when you get that way. They talk over everyone else so you can't make out the other songs and voices to hear. They're louder than them all. All except ghost cats, but ghost cats rarely show. Todds and Vixens are far more common. They talk and squabble as if they would die if they didn't. So when I heard them, I had to shut out and stop listening to the white stars and hear them instead. But I didn't want to." Louise held her head in her hands. A tear landed on her wrinkled skin. "I heard them, alright. It was impossible not to, those stupid loud termites."

Fey was even more confused. "Todd? Was that his name?" She pointed to the picture in her hand. "He was very handsome."

Louise's expression switched from solemn to angry in a flash. She grabbed the frame out of Fey's hands and slammed it face down on the table. There was a loud noise as the crack in the glass spread, breaking it into pieces.

"Argh! The lynx's ears are strong, but they don't listen!" Louise's voice quivered in frustration. She tilted the frame back up and gasped at the realization that she had broken the glass in it again. Several shards fell out into her hands and onto the photograph. She scrambled to brush them away from the picture. One of the largest shards was in the way of the man's face. As she moved it away, she sliced her thin skin on its edge. Blood seeped out and dripped on the floor.

"Oh, I am so sorry, Louise! Here, let me help you." Fey grabbed a clean tissue from her jeans pocket and held Louise's hand tight. She placed the tissue on the open wound, applying pressure to stop the bleeding. Before long, the tissue was soaked in red.

Red splotches. Polo shirt.

Fey grabbed another tissue to replace it. "Are you okay, Louise? This seems like a pretty bad cut. Do you have any bandages? Where's your bathroom?"

Louise remained unfazed. Her face showed no emotion. With her free hand, she picked up the blood-soaked tissue. "Red. Red wolves. If the white stars don't make you dizzy and the Todds and Vixens don't drive you mad, then it's the red wolves that do you in."

Fey was amazed. In front of her was a woman over thrice her age with a wound openly bleeding from her fragile skin. And still, she hadn't taken any notice at all. It was like the only thing that mattered to her were the creatures she was dreamily babbling about.

"How, Louise? How do the red wolves do you in?" Fey was anxious to hear more. Somewhere in their disjointed conversation, Louise was dropping clues. If only Fey knew how to pick them up and read them.

"Red wolves aren't like the grays and timbers. They fool you. They fool you hard into believing you're safe in their pack. They take you in and care for you like good little pups. They feed you delicious meals full of sweets and visions full of fantasy. They rock you with lullabies in their dens."

Louise swayed back and forth as if she were rocking herself to sleep, humming a quiet lullaby to herself. Then, she abruptly stopped and her eyes over-widened once again. "And before you know it, you're done fattening up on their sweets. You look down on your bowl and they've taken away the cakes and cookies and pies. Oh the pies! They're your favorite. They take it all away, including those precious pies, and replace it with something bitter and sour and much harder to swallow. But that's not the worst of it."

Louise looked at Fey from the corners of her eyes as if to check to see if she was still listening.

"I'm afraid to ask, Louise, but what's the worst of it?"

"They give you those pungent plates and they don't even have to force you to eat it. You just do! You're happy to cozy in their dens as they dress you in fur coats and clothing to match. You gobble it up as they pet you and tell you you're a good kitty. And you take it. You take it and you love it. You thank them for those nasty meals and you believe the lullabies will come again."

Louise put the blood-soaked tissue down on the table and Fey remembered she was holding her hand. "Here, Louise." She gently took Louise's other hand and placed it over the newly soaked tissue on her gash. "I think the bleeding has almost stopped. But hold onto this, okay? Press down on it. It'll keep it from bleeding too much again. I'm going to look for something to help in your bathroom, okay?"

Louise held her hands together as Fey went in search of some first aid. Louise's bathroom was in a similar state as the rest of the house. The toilet seat was broken without a lid to close. Wet towels lined the floor. Toilet paper rolls sat on the toilet tank, on the floor, and in the bathtub. Yet, there were still remnants of a composed lifestyle: a full soap dispenser with lavender scent, a fresh toothbrush with straightened bristles, and a window adorned with a green lace valance. In the corner, there was an off-white trash bin. Above the sink was a medicine cabinet. Fey opened it, hoping Louise had something in there that could help heal her injured hand. Unmarked pill bottles, an open tube of antihistamine, and a handful of yellowed bandages fell out when Fey opened it.

Perfect.

Fey grabbed a couple and tried her best to put everything else back in its place. Under the sink, the vanity doors were slightly ajar. One nearly fell off its screw when she carefully pulled it open. Inside, Fey found a small stack of towels and washcloths. She grabbed the cleanest one she could reach and dampened it with warm water. When she looked up, she found herself staring at her reflection in the mirror. For a moment, she didn't recognize herself. Her freckles sunk into wrinkles. Her skin sagged at the edges. Her eyes drooped with their lids half shut. She saw Louise in her reflection, as if she was seeing herself fade into Louise's demise in real time.

White star birds. Todds and Vixens. Ghost cats. Red wolves and bitter foods.

What did it all mean? Something told Fey that there was more to Louise's stories than what was on the surface. Somewhere within Louise was some version of the truth.

Fey found Louise still holding her hand and gazing distantly at the photo on the table. She gingerly pulled Louise's good hand away from the injury. "Here. Let's see if this helps."

Carefully, she pulled away the tissue. It had soaked through again. With the washcloth, she dabbed away at the sore. "It looks like the bleeding mostly stopped, but we still need to cover it so it doesn't open up again." Cleaning away the excess blood, Fey could see the wound better. Louise's fragile skin was ripped from top to bottom, but the deepest of it could be covered by a few bandages.

"There," she said. "Good as new."

Louise looked up at Fey with a sense of wonder. She clasped her hand over the bandages. "Maybe it is a lynx, after all," she whispered.

Fey gently smiled at her. "Louise, I'm sorry I don't understand. I don't know what you mean by that, but I'm glad you're better."

Louise reached for the broken frame on the table in front of them. It occurred to Fey that there were still several shards of glass out in the open. "You stay right there, okay? I'm going to get something to clean up the rest of this glass."

Quickly, Fey made her way to the bathroom and grabbed the trash can. She brought it into the living room. She lifted the table on its side, letting the glass slide into the bin. Carefully, she picked up what was left of the frame. She tried to fit the photo back in the best she could.

"I'd say good as new, but I'm afraid there's nothing left to hold that picture in."

Louise pressed the photo into the frame in an attempt to secure it. Her wrinkled fingers brushed the cheek of the handsome man. Her knuckle grazed at his collar as if she were straightening it for him. Somehow, the photo seemed renewed, like the image itself had life breathed into it.

"Make the choice when the time comes."

Fey looked at Louise in confusion. "Choose? Choose what?"

"Are you a lynx? Or red wolf prey? Or could you be both?"

Fey thought for a moment. She wasn't sure how to answer Louise's question. She didn't understand anything Louise had told her, even if there was a hidden message somewhere within she was trying to get through.

"I suppose if I need to be; both? Or neither? Who knows, Louise. Do you?"

Give me something. I know you know something.

Louise stared blankly in front of her without giving an answer. *Nothing.*

"Louise, is there something you know? Something you're trying to tell me?"

Again, there wasn't an answer, just a blank stare.

"Oh Louise, I wish I understood…"

Still nothing.

Fey yawned. Talking to Louise wasn't getting either of them anywhere but tired, and judging by Louise's sudden silence, she was sure she was overstaying her welcome.

"I'm sorry I dropped by so late. I'm getting tired. I'm sure you are, too. I'll let you go so you can get on with your night." Fey took herself to the front door as Louise continued to stare blankly out at nothing in particular. It was like she fixed herself in a silent daze. "Okay, well. Bye, I guess." She turned the front door handle to let herself out.

"It was Jonny."

Fey stopped in her tracks. "Jonny?" She turned around to see Louise holding the photo in her hands. She looked so sad sitting on the couch missing a cushion, in clothes that didn't fit and dirty bare feet, holding a photo of her deceased husband.

"Jonny." Louise no longer spoke out to Fey. She whispered to the photo as if she was whispering to him.

Louise Schniber might have lived in a dilapidated house. Her furniture may have been in ruins. Her knick-knacks might have been chipped and dusty. She might even have talked in nonsensical circles, but Louise was not crazy. She was a hurting widow desperate for someone to understand her. The way she looked both *in* the photograph and *at* the photograph was proof of that.

White star birds. Todds and Vixens. Ghost cats. Red foxes and pungent foods.

There was something there. Fey just hadn't decoded it yet.

CHAPTER SEVENTEEN

Fey woke up to the sound of the alarm. When her hand hit the bare sheets next to her, her memory jolted back. She would never be used to having a bed without Bruce. She stretched her arms and threw her legs over the side of the bed.

The plastic shopping bag sat untouched in the corner of her room. Fey felt as ready for her birthday as the discarded dress inside. She didn't feel like celebrating anything, not yet.

Not until I can see for myself.

She supposed Frankie had her whole day planned out for her. That was just how Frankie was. Simplicity wouldn't do.

A folding chair on her back deck faced Covista and awaited Fey with her brew. She breathed in the fresh air and enjoyed the first sip of coffee. The sour scent was gone. She took another sip of coffee and stared out in front of her. The treetop leaves seemed to glisten in the slight breeze, beckoning her. It was as if they were calling for her, inviting her into the brush and thicket.

Stay out of the forest.

Surely, Frankie would be able to escort her in and out of the woods without being "swallowed up," as Tom put it. With Frankie as a guide, Fey could finally face what she had wanted all this time and find answers to the questions that loomed over her.

After her shower, Fey wiped the steam from the bathroom mirror, except the corner of the glass. There, she drew a little heart, just like Bruce did a year ago. It was a little gesture that made her feel connected to him, still. She ran her fingers over her freckles. As she did, her fingertips found another wrinkled crease.

When did I start getting wrinkles?

Water dripped from her hair down to her shoulders. She tossed her hair forward and wrung out the excess over the sink. Frankie would want her hair dried and styled to match her brand new dress. She could hear her now. "You can't just let your hair hang like that with such a fancy dress! Why don't you let Ally fix it up for you?"

She pulled out a hair dryer and round brush. A half hour later, her hair was dried and no fancier than it felt on any other day. Fey shrugged and slipped on her dress anyway.

Despite Frankie's assessment that the dress wouldn't fit, it slipped on like a glove. She smoothed out the skirt and admired the fabric. Somehow, even though it sat crumpled in a bag for days, there wasn't a wrinkle to be found.

She reached a hand back into the bag and pulled out the necklace from the bottom. The beaded chain slinked through her fingertips and the dahlia pendant hung prominently from the middle. She easily slipped it over her head and adjusted it. The black dahlia hit perfectly at her collarbone, bisecting the dress's neckline that formed a shoulder to shoulder smile. She was dressed up, alright, just as dressed up as Frankie's pies were before digging in.

Fey filled her dress pockets with a few sticks of gum to ward off the coffee on her breath. Before she stepped out the door, she slipped the wrapper off one and popped the gum between her teeth.

Within ten minutes, Fey found Frankie greeting her with a whistle outside Spa-radic. "Look at you, birthday girl! Give me a little spin!" Frankie giggled as she watched Fey tentatively walk in a circle to the dance of her finger.

"I thought we were rendezvousing outside of the pie shop?"

Frankie ignored the question and clapped in approval of Fey's performance. "Let's get you a pedicure to match that amazin' look you've got going on! I'm thinkin' a classic French tip with maybe a diamond accent on your big toe. You'll be the envy of every foot in Soura Heights!"

Fey didn't want to be the envy of any foot anywhere. She didn't want to be dressed up and paraded down the street. What she wanted was to march into the forest and demand it to answer her, but she didn't know if she was strong enough to do that.

Fey followed Frankie through the front door. The chimes

sounded like a rattling gong.

"Do you have a reservation?"

"Two for Honey Pot."

What did Frankie just say?

"I've got you right here. I'll show you to your chairs."

Fey watched Frankie sink into a chair, slide off her shoes, and dip her feet into the bubbling water. Fey followed suit.

Before she knew it, her feet had been washed, massaged, and lathered with lotions. She looked down at her pedicure that shined back from the glossy polish. Light reflected off the tiny crystals glued onto her biggest nails.

"I'm telling you, every foot in Soura Heights is going to be jealous." Frankie clapped her hands together. "You know what else we should do?" She reached over to run her fingers through Fey's hair. "We should walk those pretty toes a few more feet to get some hair to match the rest of your look!" A little red curl dropped in front of Frankie's face. "You can't just let your hair hang like that with such a fancy dress! Why don't you let Ally fix it up for you?"

Fey took her hair into her own hands. So, Frankie didn't approve.

"Come on, Ms. Fey. Let's go take a visit to Ally. She'll know exactly what to do with that Plain-Jane hair of yours."

Plain-Jane.

The description Fey used for herself reverberated in her ears.

When they walked through the Intensive Hair doors, Ally greeted them as if she were waiting for their visit. "Oh good! I'm glad to see you girls here! Say, Ms. Fey, did you decide to get a birthday 'do today? That little birdie on your arm was sure happy to call me up and schedule you in."

Of course Frankie made an appointment for Fey.

Ally's hand quickly covered her mouth. "Oops, did I let the cat out of the bag, Frankie? You know I just get so excited when I get to have a little fun playing with hair I don't normally get to do much with."

"It's okay, Ally." Frankie's eyes lowered into slits. She didn't look amused at Ally's chatter. "Just... do a little something to Ms. Fey here, would you?" Her hand flipped in the air with a flourish. "We need this flat hair to match this pretty little dress of hers."

"Ah, I see." Ally grabbed Fey by the shoulder and guided her to the same chair she had sat in a few days ago. She pulled Fey's hair into sections to examine it. "It does hang pretty pin straight, doesn't it? Hmm... let's see what we can do. Oh, I know! Did you take a look at June's hair after she came in the other day? That short shag cut looks so cute on her, don't you think?"

Frankie rolled her eyes.

"Don't you roll your eyes at me, Ms. Frankie. She does look cute. I even got her to give me a smile when she saw herself in the mirror. A smile from June isn't exactly a common sight, so I take it she thought so, too. I don't want to hear otherwise."

Ally readdressed Fey. "So, what are we doing today? A fancy updo? Getting a curl? Beach wave? I could throw a small braid in there for you if you'd like." Ally was playing with Fey's hair as she made her suggestions.

"How about a victory roll? Wouldn't that dress up her outfit even more?" Frankie answered before Fey could get a word in.

Ally's eyebrow lifted in thought. "Yeah, I guess we could do that. You comfortable, Fey? It might take a bit to get this hair of yours to do what I want it to do."

"Sure." Fey sat still as Ally pulled her hair this way and that. Between spray, combs, and pins, her hair had never been touched so much. She felt like a turkey being prepped for dinner.

When Ally was finished, Fey looked at herself in the mirror. The face that stared back was nearly unrecognizable. Two victory curls stood on the right half of her head. It felt tight from all the hairspray it took to keep them in place. Ally had curled whatever was left down in loose curls and teased it to puff out further than she had ever seen it.

Frankie clapped her hands in approval. "Look at you now, Buttercup! I can't believe how great you look! Now it's *really* time to celebrate your birthday!"

Pleased with herself, Ally belted out a laugh. "Now that you're dressed up, what's the plan? Going to meet someone special?"

Frankie muttered under her breath, "You could say that," but before Fey could ask her what she meant, her stomach let out a primal growl. She tried muting the noise with her hands.

Frankie laughed. "I guess we should grab a bite then, huh?"

Fey meekly smiled back. "Yeah, I think I might need lunch."

"Good thing I've planned ahead."

Just as Fey predicted.

"I'll show you!"

Frankie led Fey out the door by the arm. They walked like that, with Frankie holding onto Fey's elbow and leaning on her shoulder the same way Fey used to hang onto Bruce. Together they passed all the typical people with all their typical pleasantries. Even Louise was out for a walk on Busy Street. When she saw them, her eyes grew wide.

Her arm reached out to touch Fey's free shoulder and she whispered to her, "You haven't eaten the red fox's meal yet, have you?"

"Oh bug off, Louise!" Frankie shooed Louise away with her hands, then leaned in even closer to Fey. "Don't you let that old crank ruin your day with that nonsense of hers. She's just a kook with nothing better to do than to pass her crazy onto others."

Louise yelled toward their backs, "Stay away from the ghost cats. They'll make you disappear."

Fey looked behind her shoulder and saw Louise watching back. Her eyes were wider than before and the wrinkles in her skin looked as hollow as ever.

Together, Frankie and Fey walked past the herb shop, past the clothing store, and right into the parking lot of Pie-Pie For Now where Frankie's yellow Volkswagen Beetle waited for them. The car beeped as Frankie unlocked the passenger's side door.

"Hey Frankie?" Now was as good of an opening as ever.

"Hm?"

"Frankie, I was wondering. Remember how I asked about the forest? I was wondering if maybe you could take me up there today.

Not for long. We don't have to be long, just for a little walk. Then, we can do whatever it is you have scheduled."

Frankie's hand shot up in the air. "Oh Buttercup, you have no idea what you're asking, do you?" She lifted the passenger's seat to reveal the back. There sat a blue cooler, sitting securely on the floorboard behind the passenger's seat. "Lunch!" Frankie declared with a flourish of her fingers.

Fey leaned in a little. She reached for the cooler lid for a peek. Before she could see what was inside, Frankie grabbed her shoulder and pulled her back. She spun Fey around to face her. "Just some sandwiches I made at home and apple pie with..." She rolled her eyes. "...cheddar cheese."

"A picnic?"

"I thought you might like it!" Frankie pushed past Fey to move the passenger's seat back into place. Once it snapped back, she stepped aside and gestured to Fey. "Have a seat! I think I know the perfect place to take you."

Fey took a seat in the VW Beetle. "Where are we going?" There weren't too many places to drive to in Soura Heights. Busy Street held all the businesses and the few streets around it held most of the community housing. There weren't any public parks for miles around.

Frankie reached for the dash where she kept her detachable cup holders. She removed a thermos and handed it to Fey. Fey took it from her and opened the drink valve. It smelled of lavender... lavender and something else she couldn't put her finger on.

The warm drink tasted flowery and slightly bitter. It coated her throat, warmed her, and settled her mind. She relaxed her thoughts about the forest.

"You wanted to know where we're going, Fey?" Frankie asked.

Fey looked over at her friend, whose eyes fixed on the road in front of them. Her red curls were tucked behind her ear except for the one rogue one. Half her hair was on top of her head, tied up in a red plaid bandanna. Her typical cheery disposition was gone.

The car jolted forward. Somehow, the cheery yellow car didn't feel like a charming nod to the past anymore. It seemed darker, too.

Fey hesitated. "...Sure, Frankie. Where are we going?"

The car sped up again.

"Take a look in front of us, Fey. Use that pretty little head of yours to figure it out."

Fey looked out the window ahead. They had passed Busy Street. Rosewood Court and Dover were behind them. All that was left in Soura Heights was Covista Forest.

Frankie was driving her into the forest after all.

Stay out of the forest.

CHAPTER EIGHTEEN

One Year Earlier

Fey woke up to the distant sound of the alarm, buzzing from the bedroom nightstand down the hall. She blinked her eyes open and stretched her arms out wide. She reached to wake Bruce up next to her, but realized he wasn't there. Then, she remembered she fell asleep, curled up and sunken into the couch, waiting for him to come home. Still groggy, she blinked around the room. There was no sign of him. She assumed he crept in late at night and went straight to bed, not wanting to wake her.

She stood up from her spot and rubbed her eyes awake. On the way to the bedroom, she checked in on Fern. Wet soil told her she didn't need to fill the watering can yet. She rubbed a few fronds between her fingers and slightly laughed at herself. There was never any reason to be nervous. Fern was just a growing part of their family, not some symbol of despair. She had been able to keep it alive for this long, and so far, it hadn't brought her any misery like Billy and Ol Dan.

Stay out of the forest.

The alarm grew louder. From the kitchen, it now sounded urgent. She decided to fill the watering can anyway. Even if Fern didn't need it now, she may need to water it later. Maybe if she let the alarm go longer, it would grow more persistent and actually wake Bruce up.

The alarm grew even more intense as she made her way closer to the bedroom. Usually, she wouldn't let it go for this long. There was no way even Bruce could sleep through this noise. She rubbed her hands together to warm them up. She wanted them to be ready just in case she had to take over the alarm duties anyway.

One day, I won't need to shake him awake.

Fey used the tip of a finger to crack the door open. Its hinges squeaked as she pushed it aside. She was ready, excited, to shake

Bruce's shoulder to wake him. She wanted to ask how his training went. She wanted to hear about his drive home. She wanted to offer him homemade celebration pie for breakfast while she listened to the details and gazed into his tired eyes.

But she couldn't. The bed was empty. The alarm was shouting its alert to no one.

In a confused daze, Fey walked across the room and turned off the yelling alarm.

Did he come home and leave again?

Did he already leave for work?

Did I hear him wrong? Maybe his training was supposed to last overnight. Maybe he said he would be back for dinner tonight, instead.

Fey searched the nightstand for her phone. It wasn't there.

She flipped back the sheets. Not there either.

She pulled out the drawers in the kitchen, searched the corners of the table, and flipped the couch cushions.

Where the hell is the damned thing?

Finally, she looked through the bookcase on the far wall. There it was: her phone on the third shelf. Relief washed over her as she picked it up and unlocked it. Instantly, several notifications shot up on the screen.

Fifteen percent battery.

3000+ unread emails.

New app updates.

32 text messages.

She swiped her thumb to dismiss them as fast as she could and opened her text messages. All 32 were from Bruce. She pulled up the last one:

Bruce: **Made it to the hotel for training. Get ready for celebration pie when I get home!**

Everything before that was from weeks ago, from times when he texted at work. He knew she would never check the messages, but he sent love notes to her anyway. She silently cursed herself for not at least checking it more often.

With shaky hands, she tried dialing his number. No answer.

She tried sending him a text back.

Fey: How was training? Coming home soon?

She had hoped she misheard him the night before—that he was planning to be home today instead. She hoped the reason he didn't answer his phone was bad cell phone reception.

It'll be here before you know it.

Fey helped herself into the kitchen, hoping some coffee would help wake her up, help her think straight. She opened the cupboards to find them empty of coffee grounds.

Damn it!

She slammed the cupboard door closed.

Why do we never have coffee?!

She pulled out a *Lipton* tea packet and heated a cup of water in the microwave.

She looked at the phone again. No answer.

What could I have missed?

Bruce was eager to get out the door yesterday. Did he get there late and need to stay an extra day? Maybe he had charmed his way to a couple of drinks and needed to stay the night to keep safe.

Fey went to fill the small watering can and realized she had already filled it.

He mentioned having something extra to celebrate. Was he planning a surprise for her birthday? It would be just like Bruce to plan a celebration even though they were never a big deal to her. Maybe he came home already and left to bring back a gift or balloons. Did that make sense? Wouldn't he have waited for her to wake up?

She stuck a finger in Fern's soil. It was still wet. Fey decided to turn the planter in the window.

The microwave cut off when the cup was hot. While she waited for her tea to steep, she checked Fern's leaves. They were green and lush just like they were a few minutes ago. She flicked off a piece of rogue dirt.

With the tea bag still in the water, she picked up her cup. But before she could take a sip, there was a loud knock at the door. Startled, she jumped. Tea spilled out of her cup and dripped down its side.

Shit.

She placed the cup down on the counter. Tentatively, she made her way to the front door. Maybe Bruce's car broke down and he needed to call a ride home.

"Good morning, ma'am."

Instinctively, her arms wrapped around themselves and she hugged them close to her body. She rubbed her scar with her thumb. "Good morning, officers."

Fey watched enough *Top Dog* to know when police paid a morning visit out of the blue, it wasn't to check in on what was for breakfast.

The taller man pulled a badge from his pocket and presented it to her. The shorter man struggled to present his with shaking hands.

"Mind if we come in?"

Fey held her arms tighter. "Sure," she managed to get out.

She led the two men into the apartment. She picked up her tea cup. A wet ring had formed underneath and a few drops of tea fell from the cup to the floor.

"May we?" The taller officer motioned to the empty couch. Fey nodded and took a seat in a chair facing them.

"Ma'am, my name is Officer McDonnel. This here is Officer Newton." The shorter officer looked at his feet and wrung his hands together. McDonnel continued, "Ma'am, there was an accident. Your husband was found late last night."

Now Fey's hands trembled. Tea sloshed out of the cup and onto her lap. "A car accident? He's okay, though, right?"

Newton looked up from his wringing hands. He looked confused, flustered. "No, not a car accident..." He looked to McDonnel for help.

"Ma'am, your husband was found off the trails in Covista Forest. A hiker found him and called the local authorities right away."

"The forest?" That didn't make any sense.

Why would Bruce be in the forest? His training was in a hotel in North Saint Paign.

"I don't understand." Fey's hands were wet with tea and perspiration. She wiped them on her jeans. The same jeans she wore when she last hugged Bruce goodbye.

Clearly uncomfortable, Newton rubbed the back of his neck. McDonnel continued with his calm demeanor, "Ma'am, your husband died in Covista Forest some time last night."

Died? Bruce?

Fey's heart stopped and she didn't know how to bring its beat back.

Stay out of the forest.

"No. You have it wrong. He was at a work training all day yesterday. He wasn't in the woods."

Newton had gone from rubbing his neck back to wringing his hands together. "Man, I can't do this," he whispered to his colleague. His face read of anxiety and desperation.

McDonnel ignored Newton's pleas and gave Fey a solemn expression. "I'm so sorry, ma'am. We confirmed his identity with his wallet." McDonnel nudged Newton and held his open palm out.

With shaky hands, Newton reached into his pocket and pulled out a familiar wallet. Fey eyed the B.A. monogram on the front as the wallet transferred from Newton's hand to McDonnel's. Gingerly, McDonnel handed it over to Fey. "I'm so sorry, Mrs. Anderson."

Fey took the wallet and ran her fingers over the monogrammed initials: *B. A. Bruce Anderson.* She opened it and looked inside as if anything there would bring her clarity. Cash was left untouched. Bruce's credit cards and Nonni's employee discount card were in their place.

In the left pocket, Fey pulled out the photo Bruce kept with him. Two young faces smiled back at her. He, smiling bright, showing off every tooth including the crooked one. She, laughing at him, sandwiched between two loves: Bruce, and the open book in front of her. She thought about how the park runner stopped his exercise to snap a photo. This was supposed to be a photo to look back on when they grew old together. They were supposed to reminisce when they were grandparents and argue over what day of the week it was (Wednesday) and what kind of sandwiches they ate for lunch (roasted red hummus). The photo was supposed to last a lifetime. No, two lifetimes; Both Fey's and Bruce's.

I'll be here before you know it.

But here Fey was, looking at an old photo of her husband instead of his flesh. She reached her fingers in the pocket the photo was in. Desperately, she searched.

Where the hell is it?!

It was gone. The good luck feather, the feather meant to remind her of hope, Emily Dickinson, and Bruce, was gone. She rubbed her arm again. Without the soft feather in Bruce's wallet, her scarred skin would be the only token of hope left. She felt her eyes sting, but she swallowed her tears down. "I still don't understand." She looked up at the two men in front of her. "It doesn't make sense. He left for a training event yesterday. He should have been with a group of people. At a hotel. Why would he have been in a forest?" She looked back at the photo. It had its normal crease in the center where it had been folded. But she swore she had never seen dirt smudged in the corner like there was now.

"I'm sorry, ma'am. We don't have that answer for you."

Newton looked at his colleague and spoke under his breath, "Man, we shouldn't even be doing this."

Fey shot a look at Newton. "What the hell do you mean by that? What shouldn't you be doing?"

He looked back at her, with more perspiration on his forehead. He opened his mouth, but nothing came out.

McDonnel spoke up, "He doesn't mean much by it, ma'am. Just that we don't know more than that. I'm very sorry we don't have much more information to share with you. We got a phone call from the local authorities over there early this morning. They asked us to come right away in person to deliver the news. Officer Newton just wished we had more we could give you."

Newton breathed a heavy sigh. "All we know is that they found him."

"We were on the road doing our rounds, anyway. We were

able to meet someone from over there half-way to pick up your husband's wallet to bring it to you. The officer we talked to seemed to think it might help to deliver the message in person."

Stay out of the forest.

Fey's expression grew rigid. "I'm sorry, Mr. McDonnel. How is this supposed to help? This doesn't explain anything, and it sure as hell doesn't bring my husband home to me. None of this makes sense." She swallowed hard, again, finding her voice to demand answers. "How could they find him in a forest? Nowhere near where he was supposed to be? You said 'accident'. What do you mean there was an accident? It doesn't make any sense!" Fey slammed her hand down in her lap.

Newton took another deep breath in as his hands continued wringing.

McDonnel stood up. "I'm very sorry, ma'am. We don't have any other information. All we know is what we've given you. They found your husband in Covista Forest. They described it to us as an accident." He handed Fey a card with a phone number on it. "I suggest you call this number. It'll get you in touch with Officer Brickshaw. He will have more information for you."

"And where is this Officer Brickshaw from? Where is this Covista Forest they found Bruce in?"

Fey was determined. She would call Officer Brickshaw. She would find where he was and where Bruce was found. She would ask all the questions swarming her mind. If she needed to, she would uproot her life and move there to investigate herself, no matter how long it would take.

"It's in a small town up north, ma'am. A small town called Soura Heights."

CHAPTER NINETEEN

Sitting with Bruce's wallet in her hand and no Bruce, Fey felt more alone than ever. For the first time, she could hear an unsettling quietness in the apartment walls around her. Not even the upstairs neighbors made a sound. Not that they would know the heaviness of her situation. Or, maybe they did. Maybe they had seen the county police vehicle in the parking lot. Maybe their nosy selves were listening with ears on the floor, hoping to hear a clue as to what was going on. The more she thought about it, the more she hated life in Saint Paign apartments.

She grabbed the wallet tightly in her hand. She was filled to the brim with anger that there was so much left unsaid. A ball of rage fumed inside her as a million questions ran through her mind, all of which were left without an answer.

Why did Bruce leave the hotel?

How far away was he from where he was supposed to be?

Had he been alone or was there anyone with him?

Why did two officers without any information knock on her door?

What did Officer Brickshaw know that McDonnel and Newton didn't?

How was he going to help?

Just how the hell was his death an accident?

Fey expected herself to cry, sulk in a puddle on the floor, sob for the loss of her husband, but she didn't. Not a single tear leaked from her eyes. Her emotions staggered between moments of anger and numbness. Surely, she would wake up any moment now from the couch corner where Bruce would be waiting to nuzzle into her with the scruff of his neck.

Damn it!

She picked up the card with Officer Brickshaw's number. Was

this how these things were done? It seemed odd she had to call another officer who wouldn't even bother to show his face at her door. What was she supposed to ask?

She looked down at her phone. Typical—the battery was already low. With shaking hands, she half-expected to unlock the phone to a missed message from Bruce.

No. He can't send one, remember?

Mechanically, she dialed the number in her hand. She listened to the ringing echo in her ear.

Brrrrring.

What would she say?

Brrrring.

What would *he* say?

Brrrring. Brrrring.

A male voice answered. "Officer Tom Brickshaw, Soura Heights P.D."

"Hello?"

"Yes, hello ma'am. How can I help you?"

"Um. I got your number from um… Officer McDonnel." Her voice felt weak, like it was coming from someone else's mouth.

"McDonnel? McDonnel… Oh yes, Officer McDonnel. I spoke with him yesterday, I believe. How can I help you?"

"Um. My name is Fey Anderson. And um…"

"Mrs. Anderson? Oh, Mrs. Anderson! I am so glad you called." On the other end, Officer Brickshaw cleared his throat and put on his best reassuring voice. Fey felt like if he were in front of her, he would have loosely patted her shoulder or given her a half-smile to show he understood. It wouldn't have made a difference if he had. "My condolences for your loss, ma'am. I would have come and visited myself, but I know bigger jurisdictions would rather handle house calls on their own." He loosely chuckled then cleared his throat again. "They don't like small time, small town sheriffs like me taking over their job in their territory, you know?"

Fey nodded as if he could see through the line.

She heard him clear his throat again on the other end. "Yes, well. I'm glad Officer McDonnel could deliver the unfortunate news in person. And I'm glad you called me. Mrs. Anderson-"

"Fey," she offered.

"Yes, Fey. I'd like to set a time to meet in person, if that's okay with you."

She nodded her head again and felt her focus drift away from anything that was said over the phone. Brickshaw's voice droned on about details that made no difference at all. She made an effort to write one thing down, an address to a coroner's office.

Fey's drive to Soura Heights didn't feel anything like it was supposed to. She didn't drink in the roadside scenery. She didn't notice the subtle changes from suburban housing to country roads. She didn't imagine how the tiny town she dreamt of would match up to her imagination. She didn't come up with the names of the townsfolk she might encounter. There was one concrete name she had, Tom Brickshaw, and her aim was to get to him as quickly as she could.

Her heart raced. Her feet probably did, too. She paid no mind to the speed limit signs or the cars trailing behind her. She had no idea how long she was on the road. Thirty minutes? An hour? Two? Time held no meaning. Her eyes focused on the arrow following the GPS map in front of her. She kept telling herself, "I just need to get there. I just need to go."

Time slowed down when Fey arrived at the white brick building. Her hands grasped the steering wheel as she tried to remember how she got there in the first place. She sat in the driver's seat, staring into the flat windows in front. She inhaled deeply and wondered what was waiting for her behind them. Had there not been a large printed sign in front reading **Soura Heights Coroner**, she would have thought it was just another office building, a small town bank or mortgage loan company. But behind those doors weren't front desks with smiling receptionists and candy dishes. Behind those doors was her husband's body and a stranger who she hoped could offer resolution.

She found herself in a small office room with Officer Brickshaw and another man sitting by his side behind a desk. Both men were tall, but with opposite builds. Brickshaw's broad shoulders made him appear to be the town's protector. He held himself with a quiet confidence and his expression indicated he would treat this meeting with the care of a well meaning au pair.

The second man was scrawny. His back hunched over, causing his thick glasses to slide to the tip of his nose where they barely hung on. His eyes were fixed on the ground rather than looking up at her. He wore a white lab coat and carried himself with a quiet uncertainty. She assumed he was the coroner. He seemed to be so used to death, he would have rather spent his time with the bodies stored in the freezer than with Fey in his office.

It felt cold in both temperature and atmosphere. Room decor hung around her apathetically. On the wall to her right was a round analog clock. Every third number was displayed in bold type with thin tick marks between them. The two black hands read the time at 2:15 PM. But after watching it for several seconds, Fey realized the red second hand hadn't moved at all.

Has time slowed down so much that it stopped completely?

To her right, there was an unframed poster taped to the wall by its corners. It held no color, no vibrance, and no warmth. It was simply glossy white poster paper with the word **Smile** printed in the middle. The only other thing accompanying the word was a period after it. Smile. Not an inspirational encouragement. Not a heartfelt approach to complacency. It was just a finalized statement. Smile.

It was still 2:15.

Directly behind the scrawny man was a shelf with three white-spined books. Next to the stack was an oversized print, a pen-and-ink drawing of a human skull. However, the artist took liberty with creating expression in the semi-realistic artwork. An eye socket winked and the mouth was turned up in a smile, like it knew a secret joke about death and didn't want to release the dark humor to anyone else.

It was still 2:15.

Fluorescent light from the ceiling panels coated everything in a green hue, engulfing the room with flickering sickness. Fey looked at her own hands resting in her lap and swore the color of life had faded from them. She wondered if Bruce's hands looked the same. Static-filled elevator music whispered in her ear as if it knew the dark secrets held within the beige walls. She felt as if the room around her was making her cave in on herself.

It was 2:16.

"Mrs. Anderson?" Brickshaw's gruff voice called her out of the time standstill. "Mrs. Anderson, thank you for coming out today. I know this is hard for you to do and I appreciate your taking the time to talk face to face. Can I get you anything to drink? A water or a coffee perhaps?"

Was this the southern hospitality she had been hoping for? She never wrote this side of Soura life in her meaningless, self-serving short story.

"Mrs. Anderson, on the table is a photograph. We believe the photo is of your husband, but we need your cooperation to confirm it." He pointed to a single photo faced upside down on the table surface in front of her. Fey nodded her head.

"Mrs. Anderson, you can lift it to look whenever you're ready, at your own pace. I'm not going to force you to look any earlier than you need to. There's no need to rush. But I want to warn you, what you will see may be upsetting. We chose the least graphic image possible, but there may still be some-" Officer Brickshaw paused to nail the next point home. "-distressing details. Some people find they feel better if they take their time."

Fey nodded again. She took in a deep breath, trying to hold onto the fact that her heart was somehow still beating. The stale air filled her lungs to capacity. It was like the entire place was trying to cover up the stench of rancid sweetness with artificially scented chemicals. It wasn't the fresh, open air she imagined would fill Soura Heights. She took in the room around her again. The pseudo-realistic skull mocked her turmoil.

It was still 2:16.

Her hand reached toward the downturned photo. For a moment, she thought if she never turned it over, if she never looked at its underside, this would all go away. She could go back to her apartment where Bruce would nuzzle her neck again and they would lay next to each other under the sheets, laughing about the crazy dream she just had.

She flipped it over and looked.

For the first time since she welcomed McDonnel and Newton into her home, she felt a lump grow heavy in her throat. It was unmistakable. This was Bruce. Though, the Bruce in the photo didn't look like him in any way she had seen before. His eyes lay slightly cracked open, as if he were permanently stuck in the process of falling asleep. His mouth hung wide, making him look like a fish gasping for air as its scales dried out. His head was cocked unnaturally to the side, unable to hold it steadily forward. Splatterings of darkened blood and dirt coated his temples and forehead. It had dripped down, staining his right eye the color of diluted blood. Her eyes stung as she realized she would never see *her* smile again.

It was still 2:16.

The little golden man and his horse on the white polo were now riding through puddles of dark red splatters. The photo stopped there.

What was the 'accident'?

Judging by the blood collected by his temples, something had hit him hard on his head. It wasn't obvious where his wound opened up, but from how far down it leaked, it must have been an intense bleed.

"Mrs. Anderson?"

It was now 2:17.

She blinked away any tears from falling down her cheek as she acknowledged Officer Brickshaw.

"Mrs. Anderson, I know this is difficult. Please, take all the time you need to process this, but I need your help. I need to ask you for confirmation. Can you identify the man in the photo as your husband?"

Fey nodded.

Confirmed. With a single nod, she confirmed this was reality. Her husband, Bruce Anderson, was dead.

"Thank you, Mrs. Anderson. We appreciate you coming in."

2:18.

Fey's expression grew rigid. Was that it? Did she drive out to her Wonderland only to be shown a picture of her dead husband and get shuffled away? No, Brickshaw said she could take her time, right? Then, that was what she'd do.

"What-" She clenched her jaw and felt her teeth grind against each other. "What happened?"

Tom Brickshaw looked over at the quiet coroner, who simply shrugged his shoulders at him. And as if they exchanged an understanding in their silence, Officer Brickshaw nodded in return. "Mrs. Anderson, your husband-"

"Bruce."

"Yes, Bruce. Bruce had an accident in Covista Forest."

Fey's annoyance was getting the best of her. "That's been said already. I didn't ask that. I asked what happened. How the hell can *this* be an accident?" She slammed her finger on the photo in front of her.

Brickshaw cleared his throat. "Right, ma'am. Let me see if I can explain. He was found in some overgrowth—thick trees, carpet of leaves, rocks and stumps, and the like. My guess is, he walked off the main trail and probably got lost. It's easy to lose your way out there, especially if you're not familiar with the area. Unfortunately, it's also easy to trip, fall, and hit your head out there. It's happened before. It's happened a lot before. When we found him, he had a large lesion on his head. It bled out, but ultimately he died from..." Officer Brickshaw looked over at the coroner for help.

"Traumatic brain injury," the coroner coldly answered.

"Yes, traumatic brain injury," Brickshaw echoed.

Fey looked down at the picture again. Traumatic brain injury sounded made up. It didn't sound like a real, deadly diagnosis. Traumatic brain injury sounded like Bruce bumped his head. The way his skin broke in the photograph made Fey believe it was much bigger past where the picture cut off. To Fey's untrained eyes, it didn't look like it could easily happen, not by accident.

"You're saying he hit his head? On what?"

Officer Brickshaw looked down at his hands. His thumbs shrugged in place for his shoulders. "We're guessing one of the rocks

145

or stumps nearby. We don't know for sure. We can only speculate right now."

Fey's expression begged him to go on.

"So, my speculation is that he got lost and tripped over some of the overgrown brush out there. If you saw it yourself, Mrs. Anderson, you'd see how thick some of it is. It wouldn't take much to trip and land in just the wrong way, at just the wrong spot. Unfortunately, this kind of thing happens."

Fey raised her eyebrows in skepticism. "You're telling me that my husband tripped in the woods and happened to break his fall, head first, on a rock?"

"Or a stump."

"And this rock..." Fey paused when she saw Officer Brickshaw raise a finger. "...or stump killed him?"

Brickshaw sat back in the office chair and swiveled slightly. "More or less, yes. The fall broke the skin on his head and caused swelling in the brain and tissue around it. It may help to know the chances are, he was knocked unconscious from the fall. That would mean he didn't suffer. He simply didn't wake up." He leaned forward toward her with his comforting voice. "I'm so sorry, again, Mrs. Anderson."

Something still didn't add up to Fey. It still didn't make sense why he was there in the first place. It didn't feel right. It didn't fit. "Officer Brickshaw, did anyone see Bruce before he went into the woods?"

The seat creaked as Brickshaw leaned back. "Well, I asked around and found that he stopped for a slice of pie at our local pie shop. Most of Soura Heights frequents it daily. Several of our residents said he had a plate and then wandered off to... I guess go for a hike? It seems right. Most out of towners seem to take advantage of the scenery Soura has to offer, Covista Forest included."

"But, did he *talk* to anyone?" Fey was pissed that Officer Brickshaw wasn't answering her directly. There was no way Bruce would waltz into a new town without striking up conversation with someone, anyone, around him. Surely, he told someone *something.*

Brickshaw leaned back again and crossed his arms. He looked

to the ceiling as if he were recalling the details in his own shoddy detective work. "I talked with several pie shop patrons and both of the owners. He did talk to a few people, but no one could remember anything he said exactly. The gist was this: he was just driving through and was excited to see the sites. He asked one of the owners if she knew of any open housing. He didn't stay long and his conversations were short, and then he disappeared-" Officer Brickshaw caught himself. "Well, not disappeared. I guess the forest just ate him up."

Fey sat with her thoughts, her fingers nervously twitching in her lap. From what she could piece together, Bruce left his training to visit Soura Heights. He stopped for pie.

Celebration pie? He asked about housing. Was he going to dream of houses in Soura Heights the same way he did when they drove down Mercury Lane? Was he scouting it out on her behalf? Was he there to compare it to Fey's imagination? Her Wonderland? Only to trip, fall, and die in Soura Heights? That was not how it was supposed to be. She was sure of it. Something was still off and Tom Brickshaw didn't sense it at all. He was reserved with the notion it was a pure accident. This type of thing just happened and that was that.

"So, is there?"

Officer Brickshaw looked confused. "Is there what, ma'am?"

"Any open housing?"

Fey didn't buy that her husband was just "eaten by the forest". There was something more to it, she was sure. She didn't care what it would take for her to do it, but she was going to move herself into Soura Heights and face the truth herself. Even if that meant paying for it with her own life.

CHAPTER TWENTY

Present Day

Fey felt the car gain speed under her. Frankie's foot had found its home on the gas pedal, and it didn't want to ease up. The little engine roared like a mountain lion. Fey closed her eyes, hoping Frankie was able to keep them from running off the road. She pictured June's car wrapped around a tree and swallowed hard.

Speeding in a dull Volkswagen with someone who had lost their cheerful disposition behind the wheel didn't feel right. Fey was supposed to march into the woods herself, the way Frankie had always seen her, as a strong woman. She wasn't supposed to be hurled down the road and forced beyond the trees like this.

She looked at Frankie's fixed eyes. They looked right through Fey and the road ahead and into whatever was beyond those trees in front of them.

Why are they so dark? They seem vacant.

Suddenly, Fey became very aware of the thermos she had been nervously drinking from. There was still a flavor to it she couldn't figure out. And the more she drank, the foggier she felt.

"Hey, Frankie?" Fey wanted to be careful with her words.

Frankie continued her stare out the windshield. She didn't acknowledge Fey addressing her.

Fey cleared her throat. "Say, what kind of tea did you make for our picnic?"

Frankie continued her glassy-eyed stare as she white-knuckled the steering wheel.

Fey cleared her throat again to strengthen her voice. "You're always so brilliant in the kitchen. There's no way I could create my own tea blends like you do. Lavender and..." She left her words to trail, hoping Frankie would fill in the blank.

"...valerian root," Frankie said matter-of-factly.

"Valerian root," Fey repeated. She thought back to the bag

Claire filled at the spice store.

It smells like feet and does wonders in small doses.

She inhaled the steam from the cup's valve. If she closed her eyes, she could pick up an odd scent, a bit like feet.

Frankie broke her stare out the window and shot a look at Fey. "What, Fey? You don't trust me? You think I'd poison you or something, Fey?" She grabbed the cup, took a sip from it herself, and thrust it back at her. "Is that proof enough for you, Fey?"

Fey carefully took the cup back and held it tightly. Gingerly, she drank from it again and gave a weak smile and nod.

"Geeze, Fey. I buy you a new dress, treat you to a pedicure, and get your hair fixed, and you're questioning what's in your cup? I damn near gave you a makeover, Fey. The least you could say is thank you."

"Thank you," Fey quietly thanked Frankie, afraid to say anything else.

Frankie sighed deeply. She blinked her eyes and it was as if she blinked away the dark. They were back to their typical bright blue. Her voice returned to its peppy timbre. "Listen, Fey. Valerian root is pretty cool. On its own, it doesn't smell great. But when you mix it with something strong, like lavender, it hardly even matters. It makes everything taste a little… earthier, I think. I thought it would be nice." Her wrist flipped in the air like it always did when she was casually gabbing. It was like pieces of the Frankie Fey always knew were trickling back.

Fey sipped from the thermos again. Her eyes were heavier.

"Oh. But if you have enough of it, it does have a certain… effect on you." She reached over and patted Fey's leg. "It's almost like eating a big dinner—makes you feel all nice, snuggly, and relaxed. Valerian root can do the same for you, Fey. Makes you feel relaxed. I also thought *that* would be nice for you, Fey. After all, you seem so tense on your birthday, of all days. You know, Fey, it's always something with you. You should really learn to relax a little." Frankie threw her wrist in the air again and rolled her eyes.

The fact that Frankie's demeanor softened--

Or was it the valerian root?

--made Fey relax a little. The car even seemed to slow to a normal speed. Trees rolled by the passenger window at a pace that made Fey's tension loosen up. It was like the switch she saw in Frankie switched the rest of the world around her.

Was it all in my imagination?

Fey's eyes felt drowsy enough to shut for a minute. When she opened them again, she saw they were in an empty parking lot. In front of them was a clearing with a dirt covered walking path. There was a faded blue sign that read, **Stay on the Path**.

Without a word, Frankie opened the driver's side door and got out of the car. She opened the passenger's door for Fey and motioned for her to get out. Once her feet were on the ground, Frankie motioned to the empty seat. "Fey. Move it up."

Fey lifted the seat lever and moved it toward the dash.

"Get the cooler, Fey."

Fey got the cooler. Its weight made her knees buckle a little. She was thankful even though she was in a dress with mesh sleeves and a scratchy skirt, she still chose to wear well-worn flats. At least she could still keep her footing.

"Shut the door, Fey."

Fey shut the door. The same words that plagued her thoughts echoed again.

Stay out of the forest.

"See this?" Frankie pointed to the blue sign in front of them. A curl bounced by her eye as she turned her head to read it out loud. "Stay on the Path." She turned to face Fey again. "You've never been out here, have you, Fey?"

Fey shook her head.

"Good! I didn't think so. I'm glad you thought of this, then." Frankie gave a delighted smile. "This is the blue path. You know you're on it when you see the blue signs on your hike. It's the main path in Covista. Trust me, Fey, when I say it's the one any out-of-towner needs to stick to. It's the most direct path in and out of the woods, making one giant loop back to the parking lot. A step off the blue and... well, I think you know what happens after that."

Fey nodded her head. She shifted the cooler's weight in her

hands.

Frankie smiled at Fey and beckoned her forward with a hand. "Come on, Buttercup! Our picnic spot is right up ahead." She grabbed Fey by the arm, in the same friendly way she always had. She leaned over and whispered in her ear, "Just try not to dirty that pretty little dress of yours. Okay, Fey?" Fey couldn't discern the level of seriousness in her whispered tone.

She nudged Fey to walk a few steps in front of her. Frankie led her from behind, giving her a nudge to the left or right side when needed. About a quarter of a mile down the path, Fey felt Frankie's fingers tap her in the middle of her back.

"Is this where we're picnicking?" Fey blinked her eyes around. It looked nothing like Salt Point Park. There were no tables, no clearing to lay out a blanket. This part of the path looked no different from where they had been walking. The trees and brush that lined it were left untouched by human hands.

Within the brush, Fey could hear small animals rustle. Chipmunks were searching for nibbly treats. Squirrels dodged from one fallen tree to another. Birds were flitting between branches. Something slithered between the leaves of ferns.

Ferns.

"Not quite our spot, Buttercup." Frankie's tone flipped back to how it was in the car, darkly resolute. "But we are close. Take a look over there."

Fey felt a hand guide her to the right. She turned toward the same direction. "What am I looking at?"

Frankie rolled her eyes and dragged Fey by the arm into the woods, away from the safety of the main trail, away from where the sign instructed them to stay. "Come on, Fey," she said, "Follow me!"

Together, the two women stepped into overgrown brush. Fey felt the bottom of her dress snag on the thicket around them. Tall grass and long leaves fluttered along her sides as she stepped one blind step in front of another.

On the left, Fey noticed a particular fern with fronds almost as tall as her. They were thin and bright green with an intricate pattern of holes.

Dryopteris wallichiana.

She thought about Fern at home and how it was growing over its planter and turning the kitchen into a tiny forest of its own. The fern here was a much larger version. It ominously loomed over her, threatening to wrap her up away from the world.

"Frankie…"

"Not yet, Fey."

As they walked further, Fey noticed a patch of small blue flowers by her feet. They sat close to the ground in small clusters. Fey took a deep breath and could smell a slight sweet fragrance.

"Frankie…"

"Not yet, Fey."

On the left was a fallen tree, covered in bright green moss, eating away at the dead bark and carpeting the ground around it. Fey squinted closely and saw something slide within the moss. Probably a snail. She thought about how slowly it moved through the thickness of it. She thought about how it didn't know its destination. The snail would glide along, trusting it would get to where it needed. Trusting itself the same way Fey had trusted Frankie for a year.

"Frankie…"

"Not *yet*, Fey." Frankie's voice grew deep and graveled.

Fey frowned. Frankie's Dr. Jekyll and Mr. Hyde routine was giving her whiplash. One moment she was sweet and bubble, and the next, her voice became demanding. Fey wondered what she had done to bring out Frankie's anger.

On her right, Fey noticed a patch of rocks. The largest one was in the middle, dark and pointed, leaning on its side. It was a landmark within itself. If it were a signpost, it would have read, **You should have stayed on the path**. Fey shut her eyes and focused on her senses. There was a slight trickle of water. Very slight, barely there.

"Frankie…"

"Almost there, Fey."

They walked together for a little longer. The further they walked, the more overgrown and untouched everything was around them. Her eyes would slowly blink and as they opened, she found herself stepping around fallen trees. They would close again. When

152

she forced them back open, she had to duck under branches. She had to push through brush and ignore the bugs eating at her exposed legs. She wondered where they were and why they had stepped off the main path. Weren't they going to get lost like this?

No. She said out-of-towners should. We aren't out-of-towners. She can get us back. Yes. She knows the woods like the back of her hand. As long as I'm with her. She will get us in and out.

"Here, Fey!"

Frankie stopped in the middle of a step, causing Fey to almost bump into her back.

"Here we are!" she said again.

Frankie looked around. There wasn't much of a clearing, just matted down leaves and dirt. By her feet was an exposed stump where a tree died off. There were a few rocks scattered around about the size of her fist. The sound of trickling water was slightly louder here, but she still didn't see its source.

"Here?"

Frankie motioned for Fey to sit down on the tree stump. "Yup! Here you are, birthday girl! Do you know where we are?"

She shook her head. Nothing looked familiar.

"Let me give you a hint, Fey. This is known as the red path. You see this?" She motioned all around her. "Once upon a time, this was an open path for hikers and bike riders, just like the blue trail. I would come out here for a good walk to enjoy the scenery. But then one day, they decided it was one too many paths to take care of. All of a sudden, no one wanted to keep up with it. No one would make the extra effort to cut anythin' back or clear it out. It sort of became a forgotten trail, everythin' grew over, and no one has visited it since." Frankie winked at Fey. "Well, no one except a few of us."

Fey drowsily nodded even though she still didn't understand.

"Oh, what am I thinking? Here!"

Frankie took the cooler from Fey and opened it up away from her. She reached in and took out an apple pie with cheese on top. Celebration pie.

"I knew you'd want a piece of this, Fey. Am I right?" Frankie also took out a single plate and a fork from the cooler. "This is what you asked for, isn't it?"

Fey shrugged her shoulders and tried to smooth out the skirt of her dress, noticing a few rips in the fabric.

"Look at that, Fey," Frankie scolded. "You ripped your new dress. Didn't I tell you not to do that?" Her eyes went dark again as she pulled a piece of pie away from the pan and onto the plate. She handed the plate and a napkin to Fey, but her eyes remained deadpan unfocused.

Fey accepted the paper plate onto her lap. The white napkin held the same logo she had seen every day for a year: a sepia-toned pie with the words Pie-Pie For Now front and center. The taste of apple pie filled her mouth when she took a fork-filled bite. Apple pie. Cheddar cheese. And... something else?

She took another bite. It tasted like memories. It tasted like comfort.

She took a third bite. It tasted like loss. Her eyes were fighting themselves, closing when she wasn't trying to drift off. Celebration pie was complicated at best, holding an enormous amount of feelings in a single bite.

Why do my eyes feel so tired?

She remembered the tea from the car.

Is that out of my system?

Another bite made her eyes even heavier.

What is going on?

She closed her eyes.

"Fey... Fey!"

Fey opened her eyes, just a crack.

"Fey, you awake?"

She mustered up the strength to nod her head, though her eyes still fought.

"Oh good!"

Frankie. Frankie is here. I'm so tired. Frankie is here.

Fey forced her eyes open a little more. She could barely make out Frankie unhooking the bandanna holding her hair out of her face.

Why is she doing that?

Frankie pulled up the cooler and sat down in front of Fey. For a moment, Fey was thankful she didn't have to carry it anymore. She was tired, exhausted. She knew she didn't have the energy to carry it any further.

"You see, Fey. You're not just in any spot in the forest." Frankie was getting closer to her. She leaned into Fey, close enough for her red curl to bounce into Fey's cheek. "This is my favorite place."

Fey could feel Frankie touch the back of her head and pull a blindfold over her eyes. Her eyes grew dark. It felt tight. She struggled to stay awake. She focused on Frankie's voice to keep herself awake.

"Do you know why this is my favorite place in the forest, Fey?"

Fey's head hung low, but she managed to shake it.

"Well, because it's like a little secret I share with the forest. No one travels out here, you know. No one takes a step off the main path anymore. I still remember it clearly, though. I still know this red path well, but no one else seems to even remember it exists. So, I take it once in a while on my special trips." Frankie paused a moment, then Fey could feel a hand on her shoulder. "How are you feeling, Fey? Doing okay?"

Fey's weak head bobbed in agreement.

"You see, Fey. I wanted to take you to my special place and share my forest secret with you. I don't do that with everyone, you know? Not everyone can keep a secret."

Fey's head drooped even further.

"Uh-huh." Frankie's hand moved to Fey's chin, forcing it to nod.

"Oh good. See, you're special, Fey. You're a strong woman, aren't you?"

Frankie made Fey's head nod in agreement again.

"You're such a strong woman, Fey. You had the intuition to move to our little town. Moving on with your life without needing a man by your side. Tenacity, am I right?"

Again, she forced a nod out of Fey.

"See, you're such a strong woman, I knew you'd understand.

You're special, Fey, just like Soura Heights is special. That's why you moved here after all, isn't it?"

Another nod.

"Right. And it's special because of the people who live here. See, this place right here is special, too. It's my special secret place, Fey. And sometimes, I bring people here who aren't so special. People who don't fit into Soura Heights. Do you get what I mean?"

A weak "yes" squeaked out, even though Fey still didn't understand.

Frankie clasped her hands in delight. "Exactly! It's *such* a special town, Fey! So special that we shouldn't just let anybody in it, you know? I like it the way it is, with our little shops and strong women behind the scenes. I can't have just anyone movin' in here, you know? I can't have strangers move out here, ready to disrupt our happy little town, movin' in with ideas to change things. Understand, Fey?"

Fey didn't move.

"I said, do you UNDERSTAND?" Frankie's hot breath bounced off Fey's face.

Fey nodded, trying to keep her body from falling over.

"Good! I knew you were strong all along. And you know what? It's amazin' what strong women can do when they get together. We can do great things, Fey. We can do amazin' things. Together, we can create the most perfect town. Isn't that what you've always wanted? Isn't that what you've always dreamed of? What you've written about in that cute little story of yours?"

How did she...

"But I need to know you'll stay a strong woman, Fey. I need to know that you're right there with me, like Anne and Diana, right?"

Anne...with an E?

Fey felt fingers lift the cloth from her eyes. With drowsy eyelids, she saw a red curl drop in her face. Frankie was crouched in front of her, vacant eyes staring back. "Hmm. How are you feelin' there?"

Fey could see Frankie put her finger in the pie and lick a taste. She winced. "I still don't know how you can eat that. Cheese on pie.

156

It's just unheard of. I'll tell you what, though. Those apples certainly mask that foot smell better than the tea did."

Frankie dropped the cloth back over Fey's eyes, leaving her again in the dark, struggling to keep her brain awake. She slumped over on the stump, unable to fully control her body in this sleepy state.

"Uh, uh, uh, Ms. Fey! We can't have you drifting off. Not yet!"

Fey felt her legs stretch out from under her. Somehow, Frankie was able to lift her off the stump and prop her against a nearby tree. In this position, at least Fey could lean her head back, keeping it from falling forward.

"Have you figured it out, yet? Do you know where we are?"

"In the forest." Fey cleared her throat and pushed the words out.

"Yup!" Fey pictured Frankie flipping her hand in the air with a flourish. "But do you know *where* in the forest we are, Fey?"

Fey fought with herself from falling asleep. She knew if she focused herself enough, she would be able to keep herself from drifting off. There was no telling as to what would happen to her if she did.

Where are we?

"I'll give you a hint, Fey. That idiot sheriff talked to you about it yesterday, didn't he?"

Fey's memory flashed to Tom in her living room, grabbing her arm and telling her about the body he found. The body Louise Schniber led him to.

Richard Teft?

"Someone tipped him off and he cleaned up what should have been your grand birthday present."

My birthday... present?

"I put it right here for you, Fey. You were supposed to find it. You were supposed to see for yourself, not hear it from an incompetent town sheriff. Then, I would have been able to see how strong of a woman you *really* are. Then, I'd know if I could trust you helping me to keep Soura Heights clean... free of those who shouldn't

157

be here."

Who shouldn't be here?

Leaves crunched beside Fey. She felt Frankie slide down the tree and sit down next to her. She heard her sigh and touch the end of her birthday gift dress. "It really is a shame this ripped. It dressed you up perfectly, Buttercup." Frankie paused and gave a small chuckle. "Hey, look, Buttercups!"

Fey felt her hand being forced open and something lightweight being placed in. Then, her hand was forced to close around the delicate buds.

Buttercups.

CHAPTER TWENTY – ONE

Fey's head felt like a brick was weighing it down. Her shoulders were slumped over, tired of carrying the weight of exhaustion. She fingered the substance in her closed fist. Perhaps she'd be able to keep herself from the fate of sleep if she focused on the buttercups Frankie gave her.

The damned nickname that came from a mistake.

She supposed Frankie placed them inside Fey's fist as some form of mockery, just as the pet name had always been.

Somehow, Fey mustered up her voice. "Frankie?" She felt around the ground surrounding her and touched Frankie's leg nearby. "Why did you bring me here?"

At first, there was silence. Then, "Because I needed to bring you here, Fey. Officer Dumbshaw had to go and ruin my original plans for you, but that's okay. Us strong women know how to improvise."

When Tom came to visit her, what did he say? He said he heard noises off the main trail—the blue trail. He said he stepped off the trail to get a closer look. That was where he found the body, wasn't it? That was where he found the foxes tearing away at their meal waiting for them. Fey was starting to piece together her situation.

Frankie had brought her up here, to this spot, where Tom Brickshaw found Richard Teft. His body was her birthday present.

Why would Frankie want to show me a dead body?

But Frankie did explain, didn't she? She wanted to keep the town a certain way, to keep certain people out. What Fey didn't understand was why Richard Teft didn't fit. Why couldn't Frankie just let him leave on his own accord?

Did she… kill him?

She was Soura Height's sweetheart. Everyone loved her.

Everyone confided and trusted in her. No one in town had anything bad to say about Frankie. She was their cornerstone. Everyone knew if they found themselves in any trouble, Frankie would always come running to the rescue. That was what she had done for Claire and BettyAnne when Patches was sick. That was what she had done for June when she crashed into a tree. That was what she had done for Fey when she first moved in. Frankie was always ready to be the rescuer.

Then why....?

A tiny amount of energy was left for Fey to reach up to her blindfold.

"Don't you dare, Buttercup. Don't forget, you asked for this. You asked to come into the woods, didn't you?" Frankie's voice sounded playful, but her touch was anything but good-natured. Within an instant, Frankie's hand snatched Fey's away from the blindfold. "The best is yet to come. Here!" She pulled Fey's hand into hers, interlocking fingers, the best way two mismatched puzzle pieces could. Together, they stood up as Frankie led the way.

Walking blindfolded and groggy was difficult. Fey couldn't tell which direction she needed to move her feet. She had no idea how far she was moving them. The dress tugged this way and that over the brush she couldn't see around her. Both legs felt raw from leaves and sticks hitting them with each step. Her free hand felt the scratchy whips from low hanging branches. One punctured a hole in her mesh sleeve. She felt every stab and scrape around her, but her mind was so foggy, she couldn't tell if it took them ten minutes or an hour to travel through it.

She tripped over the uneven ground. As she fell, she hit her knee on a rock. Wet warmth trickled down her leg and ran to her foot.

Am I bleeding?

"Get *up,* Fey! You're going to get that dress of yours dirty. I didn't buy it for you to rip to shreds and muddy up, did I?" Frankie continued to pull Fey through the dense forest without warning of sticks to step over or rocks to step around.

Another step forward and Fey's left foot fell into a soft spot on the ground. Again, she lost her footing and her ankle shifted at an unnatural angle. There was an audible pop. Pain shot from the spot she twisted and ran up her leg.

"Tsk tsk. You ought to watch where you're walking, Ms. Fey." Frankie pulled again, forcing her to take painful steps, limping her way through what she couldn't see.

Another pull, another wobbly step. Hair tickled her neck the way it hadn't before. Fey imagined her victory rolls were no longer victorious. They had probably let go of their fight the moment Frankie blindfolded her.

They inched along in this way for a little longer until Frankie's hand left Fey's. Without anything to keep her balance, Fey couldn't stand on her own two feet. Crippling to the forest floor, she was too tired and too hurt to walk anymore.

Frankie's voice cut through the air in a strained, sing-songy way. "We're here!"

Fey's shoulders slumped forward. She tried to lift her hands to the blindfold, but before she could, Frankie yanked it off for her. "Ta-da!" She got a brief glimpse of the fabric that had wrapped around her head—a blur of red and black.

Fey would bet anything that was a piece of Richard Teft's plaid shirt.

Fey blinked her eyes to focus on her surroundings. More brush. More ferns. More wildflowers sprinkled here and there. More fist-sized rocks and scattered branches. If it weren't for her dizzying nausea telling her she had been traveling, she would never have known she had made any progress from their last spot. Her ears picked up a sound. The trickling water she heard before was slightly louder.

Somehow, Frankie had carried the cooler along with them. The almost full pie tin sat on top. Next to the cooler, Fey caught sight of a fist-sized rock. One edge looked flat and sharp, almost like a blade.

"Where... Where are we?" Fey managed to get out.

She dug her damaged knee into the dirt, lifting herself for a better view. A small creek was right ahead. Lining the creek's bend were thousands of tiny green and red mouths.

Covista traps.

A light chattering noise broke her frozen state of fear. She followed the sound with blurry eyes. Two squirrels chased each other by the creek. One stopped and gathered a drink before continuing its race through the fly traps. Fey wished she had the same capability to run through them freely.

"Oh, just about the most special place in Covista." Frankie knelt down to Fey's level. She placed one hand under Fey's chin, lifting it forward to look directly in her eyes. "I'll give you one more clue, Fey. Want to see it?"

Fey's head drooped a little more. Feeling tattered and torn, she was tired of the game Frankie was playing. This was all some sick joke that made no sense.

"Hold on just a sec!" Frankie stood up and reached into her pocket again. "You're going to love this!" She fished around a little more, digging deep into the corners of her slacks.

Once she got hold of the item she was looking for, her eyes grew like saucers. Her dimples appeared clear as day. That curly tendril fell in front of her eyes. The way she looked now reminded Fey of how Frankie looked the first day she met her, bubbly and bright. It was like she was excited to take the world around her by the reins and lead it around with a short leash.

Frankie pulled her hand out of her pocket, threw her head back, and laughed. "Ta-da! See, Fey?" Something small was pinched between her thumb and forefinger.

A feather.

Fey's stomach dropped like lead. Frankie knelt again in front of Fey and brought the feather close to her eyes. "Get a good look, Buttercup."

Bruce's feather.

Fey's stomach turned as she thought back to the day two officers handed her Bruce's nearly full wallet. Everything was in its place except that feather, the exact feather Frankie now held onto by its quill.

Frankie twirled the feather between her fingers in front of Fey's eyes. The colors blended together in a blur. The blue of daytime sky and the gray of beginning night melted together as if time didn't make sense, and it didn't. The sky in front of her looked the same. Fey had no idea what time of day it was. She had no idea how long they had already been out. It was impossible to distinguish what was real and what was an illusion.

Hope is the thing with feathers that perches in the soul.

"Why do you have...?" Fey started to ask, but she became distracted. Frankie gently brushed the feather against Fey's cheek. Fey's heart hadn't ached so much since the day he went missing, the same day she first opened his wallet and couldn't find the feather that was right in front of her now.

"What's that, Fey? Why do I have this?" Frankie pulled the feather away from Fey and held it out close enough for her to see the individual barbs. Oddly, they were just as intact and rigid as the day it fluttered onto her open book.

"Why do you think I have it, Fey?"

By now, Fey's eyes would barely open on their own. She was so tired. She took a deep breath to intone her own mental rallying cry.

Come on, Fey. Open your eyes. See what's right in front of you. Focus. Stay awake. Stay alert. Don't fall asleep. Don't let go. Fight for yourself. Fight for Bruce.

"You... you killed Bruce. Didn't you?"

Frankie laughed. "Come on, Fey. Don't you know? The forest just eats people up, people like Bruce. I just gave it a helping hand."

Fey's stomach churned. The taste of bile crept up in the back of her throat. She swayed back and forth, half to keep herself alert, half to keep herself from throwing up.

"Why...? How...?"

"Aren't you listenin', Buttercup? I can't have outsiders in our happy little community. It just... upsets the whole feelin', you know? I don't like it. I imagine you wouldn't either, Fey. You said it yourself; Soura Heights is special. I like our happy little town, pure in its own special residents. We have our own little community and I like to keep it that way." Frankie flicked her wrist in the air. "Even Sheriff Dumbshaw has his purpose, don't you think? He keeps everyone happy enough by putting their fears to rest. We don't need anyone else comin' in and upsettin' the whole place. Once in a while, someone from somewhere else just has to stick their noses where they don't belong. They go snoopin' for a retreat from their big-city woes or somewhere to move when the fast lane life doesn't suit them anymore."

Frankie inched herself even closer to Fey. Her breath smelled of salty disdain. "A year ago to the day, your husband showed his sweet face in my shop. He sat down, excited and bright-eyed. I just knew he was trouble from the start. He was handsome, wasn't he? Well, except for that one tooth that sort of stuck out at the bottom." Frankie threw her head back again and let out a laugh. It seemed like not long ago, that laugh was gloriously contagious, full of airy delight. Now, all Fey could hear was condescending amusement.

That tooth was what made his smile *hers*. Her stomach lurched again and she threw up, narrowly missing Frankie.

"Ugh, Fey. If your hair wasn't a mess before, it sure is now. You've got puke all in it. Get yourself together, Fey. You're overreacting as usual. Anyway, he prattled on and on about his wife wantin' to move someplace quieter than... Saint Paign, was it?"

Bile floated in Fey's saliva. She gathered the taste to the front of her mouth and spat it out in front of her. Frankie moved out of the way to dodge Fey's aim. Again, she placed her hand on Fey's chin and moved her head up and down for her, forcing a nod.

"You know, Fey. He told me all about your story. The cute little one you wrote. He said it was you on a page. Isn't that just darlin'? He was convinced that if he could visit, then he could see for himself what you saw in your imagination. He decided if it compared to everything you wanted it to be, if he felt the same way you did, then he could surprise you."

"He wanted to surprise me?" Fey's head spun in circles. Was that what he had meant that day by having something extra to celebrate?

"Yup. Apparently, his new job would pay a lot more. You know, if he stayed a grocery store clerk, I might have been able to see him fittin' right in. But he was movin' up the chain. And if he wasn't satisfied with his job before, who's to say he would be satisfied with the new one? He left his trainin' and came straight into Soura to look for himself. He must have liked what he saw, too." Frankie brushed the curly tendril out of her face. Her cheeks flushed pink. "He was so… certain. He wanted to search for houses and test out the financial waters. Bless his heart, he was so naive. He believed he could build himself a corporate career and buy you a house."

Bruce wanted to buy me a house. In Soura Heights. In my Wonderland.

"I could tell he wasn't gonna give up easily. That poor boy wore his heart on his sleeve with his incessant romance." Frankie rolled her eyes. "Not that I entirely minded. That five o'clock shadow of his certainly gave him a bit of charm not even I could resist." She gave out a schoolgirl giggle. "So, I did as I always do. I listened. I listened to his whole story, but, boy oh boy, I couldn't have him just… invite himself into our little world. It would shake it up too much, you know?" Fey shook her head. She couldn't believe what she was hearing. "He wasn't even moving to Soura Heights. He was just looking." "But lookin' leads to buyin' which leads to movin' in and changin' up everything. Like I said, it wouldn't be long before that sweet-faced boy would have shook our world up. He wanted to bring his corporate mind right smack dab in the middle of our home. No, Fey. I moved to this town years ago and built up its existin' charm. I cannot let just any city kid into our neighborhood. Before you know it, the charm is gone and we've got big-name stores on every corner and streets filled with thousands of cars. No, ma'am, we can't have that, can we, Fey?"

Frankie paused and waited for Fey to answer her. She continued on when the answer was silence.

"It's okay, Honey Pot. You don't have to say anything. I know that's how you feel, too. According to that sweet-faced husband of yours, that's exactly how you felt, too. He knew you didn't like all the gadgets and buttons, not the way he did. Soura Heights was perfect just the way it was; the opposite of Saint Paign."

I'm not your damned Honey Pot! Anger echoed in her mind at the thought of Frankie, or anyone, using Bruce's nickname for her.

"So why? Why hurt someone who wants the same thing?" Fey

spat the words out like poison.

"Oh Buttercup, it wasn't something *he* wanted. That was pretty obvious. It's what *you* wanted. That's the great thing about openin' up a listenin' ear to everyone you talk to. Readin' them just becomes easy. That husband of yours may have wanted to do somethin' nice for you, but it wouldn't take much before he got bored with small-town livin' and do somethin' to destroy it."

"Bruce would never…"

"Oh, you think he wouldn't, but he was very capable. They all are. And once I saw right through him, I knew what I had to do. I had to take care of him."

Take care of him?

"You mean, like you took care of Patches?"

"There you go again about that cat. That mangy critter?" Frankie scoffed. "If I could take care of dangerous people the same way I can take care of stray cats, my job would be so much easier. No, Buttercup. I let Bruce Anderson have his fill while I listened to him prattle. Once he was done, I told him I knew just the place to show him around, to get a good feeling of the area. He wanted to see whatever it was that could make him fall in love the same way you did. And, well…" Frankie spun in a little dancing circle, her hands out by her side to present the area around her. "This is it!"

Fey felt sick to her stomach again. She could picture Bruce, blindly following Frankie, trusting the personable pie shop owner. She could picture him asking where she was taking him, blindly assuming he would walk away with the ability to surprise Fey. She pictured him accepting a snack or a drink laced with valerian root or something stronger. She pictured him drinking it up and wondering why it tasted like earth but being too polite to ask about it. She pictured him feeling drowsy, forcing his eyes to open, and when they couldn't anymore, falling into Frankie's grasp.

White polo. Red splotches.

She pictured Frankie digging into his pocket for his wallet. She pictured her looking inside it for some kind of trophy that wouldn't raise a red flag, something that would have been meaningful to Bruce but not to Tom's lackluster investigation. Her dirty fingers must have unknowingly smudged the photograph of Fey and Bruce as she pawed around in the wallet's pocket.

Pain shot from Fey's ankle, reminding her of her injury. She rubbed the sore area. Getting away with it like this might have been impossible. If she couldn't figure out how to escape from Frankie, she would end up just like Bruce. She'd end up being just another casualty the woods would swallow up.

"So tell me, Buttercup. Are you as strong as I think you are? Are you the strong woman I've seen you be before? You know, I can't do my job on my own. It's important to ask for help when you know that. Will you help me? Will you save Soura Heights from falling apart when it needs your help? Will you keep our little quaint, quiet town perfection?"

Frankie picked up the large, pointed rock from in front of Fey. The sharpened edge was aimed forward, ready to make contact wherever Frankie decided to direct it.

"Or... will you join that sweet-faced husband of yours?"

CHAPTER TWENTY – TWO

The bell rang its incessant call. Fey moved to wake up Bruce, but she wasn't the 19-year-old bride anymore. She was a 16-year-old again and in high school. The bell was the warning bell for her next class, home economics. She was nervously waiting for Bruce to turn the corner.

His next class was down another hall. It was ridiculous to think he would swing by her locker and risk being late. But there he was, a meatier James Dean *with a* Cary Grant *smile.*

Then, she was no longer in the hallway with him. She was in class, fumbling with the ingredients in front of her: apples, cheese, flour, and bugs. The bugs scrambled their way up a glass vial, constantly slipping and sliding around. Ticks and crickets and flies squirmed in black chaos.

The oven doors were open. Fire blazed out of Fey's. When she asked for help, the rest of the class stared at her, wondering what she was waiting for. She crept toward the fire-filled oven and when she reached out, her arm caught fire, but no one cared.

Bruce's face flashed in the window. The fire was gone and he was now there, holding her. Out of all the other girls in school who fawned over him, he had chosen her. Plain-Jane Fey dressed in jeans and a t-shirt.

She blinked. And her jeans were gone. In their place was an uncomfortable mesh dress. She was dressed up, as dressed up as the pies the rest of her classmates created. Bruce was no longer holding her. He was across the room, looking out the window. She called out to him, "Bruce!" And he turned, but he didn't hold his Cary Grant *smile. He didn't give her* her *smile, either. His eyes were blank and red dripped down the side of his face. Bruce dropped to the floor that was now covered in bug-eating plants. A fern draped over his shoulder.*

Fey blinked her eyes to focus. "What...what happened?" She sat up, feeling dirt fall away from under her body. Her hair splayed across her face and she could feel dirt falling away in clumps. Briefly, she wondered if she was waking up from a horrific dream, or if her mind was playing tricks on her with hallucinations.

"Oh good. You're up." Frankie's voice was deadpan. She was sitting on the ground, her knees pointed upward, playing with the feather between her fingers. She spun it slowly, playing with it the same way she had played with Fey's life.

"What... what happened?" Fey repeated.

"Well, Fey, I asked you a simple question and then you had to up and fall asleep on me." Frankie's voice still held no emotion. Fey thought she almost sounded bored.

I passed out.

Fey glanced over at the rock laying next to Frankie's leg. Its sharp edge pointed upward, threatening in its stationary position. The last time she had seen the rock, it was in Frankie's hand, aimed toward her. Fey scrambled to back herself up, distancing herself from Frankie and her possible weapon.

Frankie noticed her reaction. "Don't you worry about that, Buttercup. Like I said, I asked you a question and you never answered me. You just..." She tilted her head to the side in a mock-asleep motion, her tongue hanging out. A fake snore erupted from her nasal passages. Then, she sat straight up, laughing hysterically. "I didn't even touch you, Fey. There you go, getting all upset over nothing." Frankie flicked the feather, discarding it within the dead leaves and sticks.

As easily as she discarded Bruce.

"I've just been sitting here, waiting on you. We've been here on your time, Fey. If you could have just answered me, we wouldn't be here right now. We could be on our way back home, arm in arm, two strong women from Soura Heights banding our forces together.

169

But I've been waitin' ever so patiently for you to snap to it. And now that you have, how about it, Fey?"

"How about... what? How long was I out?" Fey looked toward the sky. Through the thick canopy, she could see the sky was darker than earlier. She had been unconscious for a couple hours.

"Long enough for me to eat what was left in there." Frankie kicked the cooler Fey had forgotten all about. "Well, almost everything. Want some more pie?" She winked at Fey. A small chuckle escaped her lips.

Fey grimaced at the thought. The taste of bile still lingered in her throat and coated her mouth, but she was thankful she didn't need to force her eyelids from closing anymore.

Frankie chuckled at Fey's reaction. "No? No more celebration pie? Well, I don't blame you, Fey. Cheese on pie is disgusting, anyway." She picked up the pie dish and dumped the remainder out onto the forest floor and rinsed off the dish in the creek. "The foxes and squirrels and other little scavengers will take care of that. They're so good at bein' the forest's little cleaner-uppers." A wink told Fey that Frankie knew those scavengers ate more sinister things than leftover pie scraps. Once cleaned, she placed the pan back in the cooler and closed the lid. Brushing her hands free of crumbs, she asked again, "So, what do you say, Fey? How about it?"

"How about *what*?"

From the moment she stepped out of the gold Volkswagen, everything was a blur. Fey couldn't remember how she got here in the first place, let alone what Frankie had asked. All she knew was that she was trapped in the one place she never wanted to be trapped in with the one person she had trusted since Bruce. From day one, Fey saw everything she loved in Bruce within Frankie. The confident demeanor. The praises to boost her esteem. Even the ridiculous pet name. Fey had always felt Frankie worked to create a bond between the two of them. But it was all mimicry to win her over. Frankie's corruption had been hiding in plain sight all this time, right where meek men and meeker women would never look.

Now, Fey could see behind the mask Frankie had paraded herself in all this time. Frankie walked her through nearly every step up to the moment she took Bruce's life. Fey felt the forest floor, the same forest floor Bruce had probably clawed at with his own hands. She had walked the same path he had walked. And now, Frankie was in front of her, pleading for her help? She needed to get out and there was no one who was going to help her but herself.

Frankie impatiently rolled her eyes. "Can I tell you a story, Fey?"

Fey shifted her weight, wincing at the pain from her ankle. She looked down and realized for the first time that she did, in fact, cut her knee wide open. Dried blood ran from her kneecap down her leg and ended in striped stains at her ankle. It was matted with dirt and bits of decaying leaves. A hungry fly buzzed around it, attempting to lap up the remaining fluid from her wound. She swatted it away only to watch it meander to the creek bend where a flytrap swallowed it whole.

"Sit down and stay a while, Fey," Frankie joked. "It's not like you have anywhere to go now." She shifted her own weight so she could sit on her knees directly in front of Fey's line of sight. This made Fey feel even more trapped. Frankie's red hair swung in front of her hungry eyes. It was like she was wounded prey and Frankie was… What was Frankie?

Red wolves.

It was like she was a red wolf, circling her mark, batting it around in play until she decided how to finish it off.

"Do you remember the day you moved here? You came into my shop, just as timid as could be. I remember you lookin' lost, but it wasn't like you couldn't find your way. You were determined to get through it. You weren't going to stay, were you? You were going to grab a slice of pie to go. But that's not how I work things, is it? No, ma'am. If you come into my shop, you're going to have a seat. You're going to order a stinkin' pie and tell me your story." Frankie reached over and played with a tendril of hair by Fey's face. "You were an outsider, but I could tell right away you were different. You weren't the bright-eyed, bushy-tailed outsider looking for a quick retreat only to discard it later. You weren't some kind of interloper trying to rip apart our special place. It didn't take much to convince

171

you to sit down and have a chat. You welcomed the company, just like Bruce did. But you were different. You fit right in."

With the meek women.

"It's like you didn't aim to tell me everything, but it just... spilled out. Everything from how you imagined our tiny little town to Bruce's 'untimely' death. I almost felt sorry for you, really. I counted your tears. You shed six that day. That takes some guts, you know? Cryin' in front of a stranger. But you did. And I remember how torn you were to tell me much of anythin', really, but slowly and surely you let me in that pretty little head of yours."

Frankie tapped Fey's forehead. It reminded her of when Bruce complimented her brain, but coming from Frankie, it felt like an insult.

"You know, your face was familiar that day. That sweet little face. Only, it was a little older than I thought it would be in person and a little sadder. Still, I recognized your face. Freckles, pin straight hair, eyes that told me you liked to hear a good story. I guess it was from that silly wallet photo he had on him." Frankie rolled her eyes again and shifted her position. She lay her back against a tree and settled into a comfortable stance. She gave a sigh that said she was bored with her own story. "Within a few weeks, you earned yourself a cute little nickname and decided to run errands for me. You, my dear Fey, my Honey Pot, you are the very definition of a strong woman. We could be strong women together, you and I. Do you have any idea what we could accomplish if we worked together? Put our strength together? Our tiny little Soura Heights would be everythin' you imagined in that cute little story of yours. It could be satisfyin' perfection. That's how it goes, right? Isn't that how you wrote it?"

The only response Fey could give was a blank stare. Bruce must have told her about her story, her silly Wonderland story that never had an ending. The one that was just for kicks for herself and no one else. He must have let his ridiculous nickname for her, Honey Pot, spill out in conversation. He must have mentioned his love for gadgets and how it made Fey anxious to get dragged in and out of electronic stores. And Frankie must have logged all those details in her head to call back later when it would convenience her.

172

"Anyway, I made sure you weren't gonna invite anythin' devastatin' from that horrible stacked city you came from. I figured you couldn't do *that* much harm if you stuck around. So, I made sure you did." Frankie's voice was peppered with insolence. "June and I agreed, you'd be an excellent addition to our little group."

Fey looked up at Frankie, shocked. "June? What does June know about all this?" Sure, June was quiet and brash in her own way, but Fey never saw her as dangerous. It seemed unlikely she had her hand in some insane plot to rid the town of anyone who didn't 'fit'. Then again, Frankie never seemed like she would have, either.

"Haven't you noticed how strong she is? She can hold her own over at Pie-Pie For Now without any help. I've trained that girl right. She listens well. Well, usually she does. She did get that stupid haircut. But not you. Look at you with your pretty hair and your pretty dress. We just need to teach you to take care of your things a little better. But that can be done. With you by our side, I know we can do even greater things. Like I said, it's amazin' what strong women can do when they get together."

Fey swallowed her dread. If June was doing Frankie's bidding, who else was in on this insane plot to bubble their town?

"What about Claire?" Poor BettyAnne. She hoped the sweet little girl wasn't caught in the middle of this sick game Frankie orchestrated. The idea that little BettyAnne would grow into her years believing this was normal. "And Katrina? Ally?"

"Those nitwits? Nah. They're born and raised as weaklin's in Soura. They're okay enough, they're not goin' to spoil anyone's fun here, but they certainly couldn't handle bein' besties. Not like you! Am I right?" She nudged Fey's shoulder in a joking manner.

"And Tom? What about Tom?"

"Like I said, Sheriff Dumbshaw almost ruined things for us. But he won't be a problem. See, the great thing about being a great listener is that everyone wants to tell you their story. Everyone lets you in on their secrets. And your buddy Tom isn't any different. He just isn't the brightest crayon in the box. He's just a small-town boy who believes the best in people. Years ago, when I bought out Pie-Pie For Now, I sweetened him up with a specialty pie. It only took one bite and he was happy to lend me a helping hand, on duty or not."

Frankie leaned into Fey, eyes dark and glassy. "Want to hear another story? It's a doozy. See, I always had the image of this town in mind. Growin' up on Dover, I got to know everyone here. They were kind, sweet. No one batted an eye because no one stepped outside of the rules. But then one day, Mr. Jonny Schniber got a bug in his pants."

Jonny.

"He pulled me aside and told me about some big plan of his." Frankie threw a pebble out in front of her. "He was gonna hire some people to come in and pave over the whole place. He was going to bring in more people. Build it up. Turn our little town into a city. Can you believe that?"

The image of Louise's aged photo broke into Fey's mind - the young, mustached man on Louise's arm, holding onto young love and life.

"I told him he couldn't do that. He'd be destroyin' everythin' we ever loved. All of us born and raised Soura-inites." Frankie shook her head. "I thought if I could take him out, you know, show him the scenes, I could talk some sense into him."

Frankie flipped her hand in the air. "So we went on a little hike, right out here. But he kept yappin' his mouth about bigger things. And then he pissed me off. He said, 'Frankie, you don't get it. I'm gonna make this town what it should be.' If anyone didn't get it, it was him. So I pushed him." She shrugged her shoulders. "I pushed him and he fell. It wasn't until I offered to help him up I realized he hit his head. I thought he was foolin' me somethin' bad. He wasn't movin'."

Frankie shook herself of the memory. "I don't regret it or nothin'. It saved Soura. And I grew strong. I brought ol' Tom a pie and told him what happened. He said it was an accident and told me he'd make sure everyone would stick to the safest trail out here. That's when they blocked off this old trail and let it grow out. They thought if they kept everyone's feet on a main trail, they'd prevent it from happenin' again. And it would have, if everyone had kept in line. But all it would take is one wrong step off the trail and anyone who didn't know their way around could just get eaten up. The day after he told me that story, a man came in talkin' about wantin' to pave over our wooded areas and build a nasty shoppin' center full of unneeded junk. He was gonna tear the town apart. Could you believe it, Fey?" Frankie's eyes widened as she posed the question, but she didn't give any pause for an answer. "No more charmin' Busy Street. No more small business owners. No more quiet walks with friendly faces. All the reasons I moved here, all the reasons fate brought you here, it would all be replaced. You know, Fey, I should really give some credit to Tom. He's the one who gave me the idea."

Fey shook her head. "How... how many, Frankie?"

"How many? How many have tried to ruin our little community here? How many have tried to eat it up themselves with big city corporate ideas? Oh... let me see." Frankie blew the curl away from in front of her face. Her eyebrows furrowed, annoyed that it fell back in defiance. She looked up to recall her memory. "I think we've counted at least thirty."

Fey's head went light at the sound of the number. Thirty. Thirty people have walked into Soura Heights never to walk out again. Thirty people who may have had big ideas, or simply big mouths, sat across from Frankie's eager ears. Thirty people who may have just been passing through never made it out. Thirty people ended up fallen in Soura Heights. Fey didn't know if Frankie was telling the truth or embellishing. It didn't matter. Either way, Fey's stomach was in full knots. It seemed Frankie lumped people into two categories, fit or unfit, and Bruce fell into the same category most people outside of Soura fell in: unfit.

Thirty. Bruce was just one of thirty.

Nothing was going to change that. Nothing would bring him back.

"So, Ms. Fey, story time is officially over." Frankie looked up through the treetop canopy and into the sky. "Now you've had a chance to hear me out, you've had a chance to think about it. How about it? Are you strong enough? Are you a strong woman like I've always thought you were?"

How the hell do I answer that?

175

Fey had no idea what to say to the woman in front of her. This was the same woman she trusted since day one of Soura Heights, the same woman she ran to in need, the same woman who assured the entire community she was devoted to creating a place of comfort and solace. And she was. There was proof she was in her gnarled story. In her own twisted way, she was just as devoted as she appeared.

Fey closed her eyes. She thought of Bruce. What would he say if he were alive?

"You're right, Frankie. Strong women can do amazing things, can't we? We can do anything we set our minds to—build a career, pack our lives up and uproot wherever we want, start a new life over. We can own a business and build families. We can construct relationships with the people who suit us. A strong woman can even build an entire life, an entire town, in their own image, if she wanted."

Frankie nodded in agreement. Building a life, a town, in her image was exactly what she was doing.

"But you forgot one thing about strong women."

As painful as it was, Fey pulled herself onto her knees and crawled over to Frankie, facing her the same way she was faced moments ago. Her open wound stung as her knee dug into the dirt and mud.

"You've got one thing wrong, Frankie. Unlike me, you are no strong woman. You are a coward. You hide behind a fake persona, tricking everyone into trusting you as some kind of town leader. But you are just a scared phony. And you've used your fear to fuel you in the most cowardly way possible. Let me tell *you* a little story. You remember the day I moved in. You tell it well. True, I felt comfortable talking with you. Partly because you seemed to care, also partly because I needed someone to care. But I didn't tell you everything. I knew Bruce's death was no accident. I could feel it. That's the funny thing about having a *real* connection with someone. You just know when something is off. Something never sat right with the idea that the forest simply ate him up. People don't just disappear for no reason. I didn't come here just to live out some fantasy I created on paper. That dream left me the same day Bruce did. It disappeared right along with him. No, I came here to find out what really happened to my husband. I came here to see who was behind this so-called 'accident'. I knew, once I could swallow my nerves and get into the forest, I'd figure it out." She grimaced at the infection she was no doubt giving herself by crawling through the dirt with an open wound. "I just didn't plan for it to happen this way."

Fey inched a little closer to Frankie, until their noses almost touched. Frankie's blue eyes were dark again and her curl brushed against Fey's eyelashes.

"No, Frankie. I'm not going to join this sick little gang you're trying to form. I'm not going to blindly follow you in this fight you decided to create. It's taken me until now to truly believe it, but I am strong. And I'm stronger than you, Frankie, because I'm deciding right now I am no blind follower. But I have to thank you because I don't think I would have stepped foot into Covista without you dragging me along. Now, I can look at you in the eyes and do what I came here to do a year ago. I can get some justice for Bruce."

At that moment, for the second time in 24 hours, Fey went unconscious.

CHAPTER TWENTY – THREE

A fly buzzed around Fey's ear. "It'sssss hereeee," it hissed in her ear. "Dinner isssss here." Though, there was no plate in front of Fey. But the fly wasn't talking to her, was it? It was calling out to the plants around her, and the Covista traps heard it.

Fey's leg was frozen in its spot. A flytrap had walked its way from the creek bend and toward her limbs. It had wrapped itself around her leg, preparing for its final attack. One of its mouths already had hold of her foot, wrapping its plant-teeth around her, gnawing away from her pinkie toe inward.

A second mouth crept forward. It weaved in and out, like a snake assessing its kill. It stopped inches away from her face and opened wide. It smiled, happily taking in the sight of its next meal.

And then, two other mouths whipped to either side, grabbing hold of each arm. The big one licked its lips and lunged forward.

"Hssshsshss," the fly laughed. "A dinner prettty enough to eeeeat."

The plant was eating her alive, swallowing her whole, claiming her as one of the fallen.

Fey felt as if a bomb had gone off in her head. She opened her eyes, grateful for the murky gray light. There must have been a bright moon somewhere above the trees.

Moaning, she lifted herself on her elbows, realizing she was on ground, not floor.

Damn it, Frankie.

Sending her fingers to explore the back of her head, she

178

winced. The tacky consistency of blood matting her hair told her she had been unconscious for... at least another hour. Memories of the day flashed before her. The pedicure, Ally's hair salon, Frankie pulling her into the forest.

Where the hell is Frankie?

Frankie had left her there to die, but Fey couldn't waste time feeling sorry for herself.

With her good foot, she shuffled to the nearest tree and hauled herself on her feet. A step forward and she toppled to the ground. She swept her hands along the ground and found herself a branch sturdy enough to stand as a crutch.

Now on her feet, Fey could hone her senses to figure out a plan of action. Her ears perked up at a loud *to-wit-to-woo.* A nearby barred owl called out again. This time, it sounded more like *Who Cooks For You?*

Shivers prickled the nape of her neck. She could still taste pie mixed with bile in the back of her throat.

The forest just "eats them up."

If only she had listened to the warning that rang through her ears. If only she hadn't been so determined to find out the truth of what happened to Bruce. Stepping into the forest may have given her the answers she needed, but now she was stuck wondering if she'd become one of the fallen.

Come on, Fey. Get it together.

She steadied herself, finding the best way to hold the branch. She focused again on the sounds around her, hoping for a clue on where to take her next step. She heard water.

The creek.

There was something there. Something moving. The animal heard her inch closer and whipped its head around.

It's just a fox.

Its bushy tail twitched and then it darted away, chattering to itself.

Todds and Vixens.

Suddenly, Fey remembered another book from her childhood, one she slept with under her pillow when she was no older than five or six. Its cover flashed into her memory: a dapper fox in a tailcoat and cane. *The Tale of Mr. Todd* by *Beatrix Potter*. Even in a scramble for life, books still showed up for her as a way of clearing her perception.

That's what Louise meant, isn't it?

Louise wasn't talking in nonsense circles at all. The Todds and Vixens she was talking about weren't imaginary creatures, they were foxes; bushy-tailed scavenging foxes. She said they were singing their song loudly. What did that mean?

Didn't Tom mention foxes?

When Tom came over that night, he said he heard a couple of foxes fighting over a meal...over Richard Teft.

The songs of Todds and Vixens were the foxes fighting over their food. When Louise heard them, they must have been fighting over Louise's husband's body, over Jonny. The same man whose death gave Frankie her grand idea of keeping the cloth of the town clean from interlopers.

Fey used her branch-crutch to move forward. All she had to go off of was the sound of the running water. She had to walk away from it enough to barely hear the sound.

Who cooks for you? The owl hooted again. Her stomach growled and her mouth felt dry.

Fey shook herself of the thought. She couldn't stand still. If she did, she would end up with the same fate as Richard Teft and Bruce. She forced herself to keep moving.

As she hobbled along, she felt something behind her. She turned around, but there was nothing. A few feet further, and she felt it again. The hair on her neck stood on end. Again, she turned around and there was nothing.

Damn it, Frankie and your fucked up plans.

She hobbled faster, ignoring her injuries, focused on moving, on getting out. And then she heard it clearer. It was like soft feet padding through the dead leaves behind her. Slowly, she turned around. Right in front of her stood a mountain lion, crouched in anticipation. It must have been stalking her without a sound.

Ghost cat.

Fey's heartbeat escalated as she tried to recall anything in literature that might help her walk away. She took a step backward. The cat inched closer. She could see its silver whiskers twitch by its mouth. As she took another step back, she felt a branch touch her hair. With one hand, she broke it off the tree and held it out in front of her.

"Get back!" She swung it out like a sword.

The mountain lion responded with a low, guttural growl.

"Get back!" She commanded it in an authoritative tone.

The lion inched forward again. Its growl grew louder and morphed into a quick roar.

Without bending over, Fey kicked a rock at it. "Get!" She swung the branch again, in the same movement Bruce used to, but bigger. "Get! Get back!"

Fey's heart rate echoed in her ears, and she watched the ghost cat refuse to back down. It roared again and she could smell its breath. It was as real as her imagination had made it out to be.

"I said leave me the hell alone!" Fey took a commanding step forward and threw the branch. It hit the side of the lion's head, making it twitch its ears in annoyance.

"Go find something else to eat, you ghost cat!" she commanded with another step toward the cat.

The lion twitched its ears, growled again, and slunk away into the shadows.

Fey grabbed her chest. Her heart was slowing, but it felt like it was going to burst through the constraints of her dress at any moment. Once she was sure the mountain lion was off to stalk something else, she turned back around and kept herself moving.

Damn it. I am *strong. If I'm strong enough to ward off a mountain lion, I'm strong enough to face Frankie when I find her.*

CHAPTER TWENTY – FOUR

Fey felt a ball of guilt in the pit of her stomach. Her chest heaved forward and mouth shot open. A salted sour taste filled her mouth as she vomited anything that was left in her already emptied stomach. Bruce had always kept Fey safe from the forest in her imagination, yet she was unable to keep him safe from the one he walked right into. Her hands touched the dry leaves in front of her. She clenched down on her jaw and balled her fists. The leaves she held onto crumpled into bits.

For the first time since McDonnel and Newton visited her a year ago, she let out a guttural wail. Her body shook. Tears poured from her eyes in puddles that ran down her cheeks. He didn't deserve it. Fit or unfit, he didn't deserve to die. He didn't deserve to take his last breath on the same leaves she found herself fallen in.

Fallen. They've fallen again.

A second heave brought up more bile. There was nothing left to vomit. Bruce may not have been able to walk freely from Frankie's trap, but Fey would be damned if she wasn't going to fight herself.

Before Fey knew it, she had come across a familiar stump. The very same stump where Frankie sat her down and fed her the dubious celebration pie. In hindsight, she wished she had fought back then. She wished she could have been Chuck Norris and tackled Frankie to the ground.

She continued to shuffle along until her makeshift crutch hit something hard. She looked down and saw the leaning rock. Now, if it were a sign, it would have pointed her out of the thicket while yelling, "Run!"

Fey felt her face grow hot. She swallowed to keep herself from dry heaving again. It had all been an illusion to keep Fey right where Frankie wanted.

Then again, Frankie had given her exactly what she asked for, didn't she? She showed Fey the exact point where Bruce's life left his body. Actually, she did more than that. She walked Fey through the exact steps she took to take Bruce's life. She explained in detail her motivation and knew how the only person who should have kept the town safe from her, Tom Brickshaw, would brush it off as another accident. She had tricked Fey just like she tricked Bruce. Just like she probably tricked Richard Teft and God only knows who else.

It wasn't long before she heard another sound. This time, it was steps. At first, she wondered if the mountain lion was back to reclaim its prize. But these steps were different from before. They were deliberately rhythmic human footsteps.

Fey's heart raced excitedly.

Someone is coming!

Hope was with her again. She held her free hand in a tight fist, as if she were holding onto the hope feather that had already been long lost. If only she could alert whoever it was, they could get her help. She wouldn't have to guess her way out of the dark forest on her own. They could walk her to the main path and drive her to get medical attention. She could leave all the flytraps and sycamores behind her.

With that thought, she picked up her shuffled pace. She ignored the throbbing from her ankle, telling herself to *move*. The walking sounds came closer. Now, it sounded like more than one person. The idea made her heart jump twice as fast. Whoever decided to take a late night stroll in Covista couldn't have chosen a better time or place. She was glad whoever it was decided to step off the main path and explore the long deserted one.

Through the thicket, she saw two faint lights. Flashlights. She shuffled quicker and quicker, eager to chase these people down, grab them, and thank them for their rescue.

But that eagerness came to a halt when she heard their voices.

"Of course I remember where. This isn't my first rodeo, you know!"

It was Frankie.

"Obviously, but we need to be sure."

And June.

Fey's heart beat faster, but not out of excitement. There was no way she could let the duo find her wounded and helpless. They could easily overpower her. It wouldn't take much for two strong women to finish off a wounded animal.

She picked her branch crutch off the ground and pulled it waist level. She had to find a place to hide. The only place close enough was a large sycamore tree. Leaning on its bark, she scooted herself around to the opposite side and slumped to the ground. With eyes closed, she hoped their flashlights wouldn't find their way to her direction.

As their voices grew closer, Fey kept her eyes on their flashlights. The light danced through the brush in line with their steps. Left. Right. Left. Right. They barely struggled through the overgrowth and stepped around every obstacle with ease. It was as if Frankie and June had memorized the woods from traveling this path several times before. They knew its intricacies and anticipated its hurdles.

Before long, both women stopped within Fey's reach from the tree. They were directly on the other side of the rugged tree trunk. Fey could hear their feet shuffle in place, adjusting themselves in small circles. Leaves crunched under their feet so close to Fey, it sounded as loud as broken glass. If she wanted, she could have reached out to tap their ankles. She didn't move. She held her breath and imagined herself as small as one of the crumpling leaves under Frankie's feet.

"What's it now, Ms. June? Why are you stopping so sudden?"

"Something's wrong."

Fey imagined Frankie's eyes rolling. "Come on! There is *nothing* wrong, Ms. June. You're just paranoid. You're overreacting. Look around."

As Frankie shined her flashlight in a circle around her, Fey shrunk herself as small as possible behind the tree trunk. She closed her eyes tight and imagined herself tinier than a crumpled leaf, tinier than the dust it collapsed into.

"It's the same ol' Covista it always is, June. The same

overgrown red path. You oughta know it like the back of your hand by now, don't ya? Or, June, do I need to give you a little refresher?" Frankie's voice sounded like she was delivering a threat. It was the same tone she gave Fey when she held that sharpened rock in her hand.

"No." June's response was flatter than the earth under all the scrub. Fey thought she saw her head droop toward the forest floor. For the first time since Fey had known her, June sounded and looked defeated.

"Don't you forget what you promised me, June. After I saved your tail from that awful car crash you put yourself in, you remember what you said?"

With her eyes aimed at the forest floor, June nodded.

"You said, 'anythin',' didn't you, June? You said you'd do anythin' it takes to keep our Soura safe, just like I keep you safe." Frankie flipped her hair out of her face. "And to do that, you have to trust me, June. Trust me, I know what's best for our little town."

June silently nodded again and slowly drew her head back up.

"Okay, then! So it's settled. I'll show you, June, she's just as gone as the others. She simply wasn't strong enough to handle an agreement with us."

"Strong enough?"

"Yup! That girl wasn't strong like you, June. You've got a tight lip and a sworn friendship. That's exactly the kind of girl I need by my side. I thought she would do us good, June, but I was wrong." Fey could see Frankie's hand run wildly in the air, the same way she always did when she held nonchalant conversation. "She just couldn't handle it. And now, you don't have to worry your pretty little head over it anymore, June. Sooner or later, someone will find her there and she'll be another out-of-towner who just lost her way in the woods. How is it that Tom puts it? Oh, yeah. 'The forest just eats people up.' That's what he'll say. 'It swallowed her whole.' And we'll all put on our sad little faces like we always do and keep on our merry ways. Right, June?"

Somewhere in Frankie's speech, June found enough confidence to dust off the defeat and move on. Fey could see the

185

outlines of their bodies walk past the tree she was hiding behind and to the area where Frankie left her for dead. Quickly, she scooted around to the front of the tree while their backs were turned, their lights fading in the distance. Without hesitation, she lifted herself from her post and stumbled forward.

It wouldn't be long before Frankie and June would realize Fey wasn't face down in the brush without a heartbeat. Once they detected the empty spot of land, they would turn around and search for her, like hunters after prey.

With no time to lose, Fey shuffled quickly forward. She didn't know where she was going. One foot after the other, she blindly made her way in the only direction she could: forward. In her hurry, she tripped over something. Her ankle nearly gave out from under her again. Taking panicked breaths, she recovered her footing and moved on. It didn't matter what shape her body was in, she had to make it go. It was her only option.

But then she heard their voices behind her again. They were making their way back. They realized their mistake earlier than she anticipated. She had thought it would take them just as long to get there and come back as it took her to reach the tree she had hid behind. But then, she had forgotten they knew their way around while she didn't.

The second she heard them, she dropped to the ground. On her hands and knees, she crawled until she came to large, wide leaves hitting her face. She knew the shape from years of caring for Fern with Bruce. Fey crawled along the fronds and sat in a fetal position, her hands wrapping her knees. The leafy fronds draped over her like blankets protecting her from a storm.

Fern, please protect me.

Two flashlights shined frantically through the forest as they approached her.

"Buttercup!" Frankie called out her nickname for Fey, drawing it out as if she were calling for a lost puppy. "Butttter - cuuuuup!"

Fey crawled inside herself even more with shallow breaths. Frankie's voice was like the mountain lion's roar before it pounced.

"Oh, Buttercup!" Frankie was again unknowingly within a few feet of Fey. She stopped calling out and addressed June in an annoyed tone. "I swear the girl is just so *stubborn!* I left her there, I know I did. She wasn't movin' when I left, June. I even double-checked after I cleaned up. She couldn't have gone far. Today's rock was extra solid. I thought it would do the trick nicely."

"I guess it didn't." June's dull voice broke through. Fey couldn't tell if she was being sarcastic.

Frankie's light darted toward June's face. "No. I guess it didn't, did it? I won't make that mistake again, Ms. June. Understand?" With the light on June, Fey could see her expression drop. Her eyes narrowed to the earth. Her lips turned downward. She clenched her jaws tight and swallowed.

The two women made their way closer, calling out for Fey once again. "Oh, Ms. Fey! Where are you? Are you doing okay out here?"

Fey rubbed her ankle, then the back of her head and wondered what "okay" really meant anymore. She felt the fern leaves move behind her, but not from her own movement. Frankie had inched herself closer than Fey realized. Her feet were on the opposite side of the plant. If she moved a few inches closer, she would step right on top of Fey.

"Feyyyy-yyyyyy!" Frankie dragged her voice out again and it rang in Fey's ears.

Fey's options were limited. If she ran, Frankie would catch her before she could get far at all. There was no question, Frankie knew these woods by heart and Fey could barely get by.

A single step backward would be all it would take for Frankie to find out Fey's hiding place if she stayed curled up in the same position. Judging by June's disposition, there was a wild chance she may betray Frankie if Fey gave her a reason. Even so, there was no catching June's attention without Frankie knowing. Could she find a new place to hide? Probably not. There was no way she could move around swiftly enough to go unnoticed.

There only seemed to be one real option. She gently moved her hand out to grab her branch crutch where she left it on the ground.

She curled her fingers around the bark and gripped tight. Her heart felt like it was going to beat out of her chest. Sweat dripped from her forehead and beaded into her tarnished hair. She pulled the limb closer to her and readjusted her fingers, doing her best to keep her breath controlled. One wrong move and she would end up fallen like the rest of them. Fey waited for Frankie to call out again.

"Ms. Feyyyyyy!" Frankie turned her flashlight to face June. And at that exact moment, Fey swung out the branch into Frankie's ankles. There was an audible crack. Fey's own ankle felt relief at the sound of Frankie's fresh injury.

Surprised, Frankie fell to the ground with a gasp. Her flashlight landed in a soft thud. It rolled off to the side within reach and covered itself in dirt and leaves. At first, she was still, stunned into inactivity. Then, she grappled with where to put all four limbs. There was a distinct sound of fear in Frankie's labored breaths. For once, Frankie didn't have the world wrapped around her finger. For once, she was on the other end of the string and didn't know how to take it.

In the darkness, Frankie kicked out her feet. Her aim was anywhere. Her shoes landed in repetitive blows on Fey's ribs. Each jolt took away another of Fey's breaths. Fey held the branch crutch out in front of her as if it were a shield protecting her from a blade. With each hit, the limb grew slightly weaker. Within seconds, the kicks subsided. As Frankie gathered her breath, Fey made the calculated decision. She instinctively reached in front of her and grabbed at an ankle.

"What? Is that... Is that you, Buttercup?" Frankie's voice struggled to regain its assurance. For an entire year, she held power over Fey. She built her up, calling her strong, patting her on the back. Frankie took her in, dressed her up, and fed her. Fey thought it was all in the name of friendship.

But all along, Frankie had treated her like one of her pies. She dressed her up and displayed her on a plate to be fed to the forest. Fey wasn't going to allow her to hold any power over her any longer. She didn't answer her, not verbally. With her hand on Frankie's ankle, she pulled her closer.

At the same time, Frankie took hold of her flashlight and shined it directly in Fey's face. Briefly, Fey saw Frankie's expression, a maniacal smile and eyes open wide. Without looking, Fey reached beside her and grabbed hold of the branch. She could feel the bark around it had weathered away. A few more uses and it would easily break into pieces. She strengthened her grip and transformed its function. With a newly held grasp, the branch had transformed from a crutch to a shield, and now to its latest use: a club.

Frankie pulled herself forward, sat up, and leaned in close to Fey. She could see the outline of her face and feel Frankie's heavy breathing. She thought she could hear Frankie's lips part into a smile.

"Oh Buttercup," Frankie whispered. "It is you, isn't it? Well, I'll be damned. You're a totally different breed all of your own, aren't you?"

Fey tightened her hold on the club some more. She wanted to make sure she had it right. It wasn't time, not yet. She had to hold her patience first.

"You sure aren't that timid little girl I met a year ago, are you? In fact, I think I was a little right about you after all. You are strong. Look at you, you're up and runnin'. Like a little Energizer bunny, you've kept going. And now here you are..." Frankie paused and she inched closer. She called out to June, "You see this, June? She really is strong after all." But there was no answer from June. Then Frankie's voice dropped to a low whisper. "It really is a shame that sweet-faced husband of yours was just swallowed up like that. I'll do you a favor, though. I'll make sure you join him right here." Frankie's head tilted back and Fey could hear her laugh toward the cloud-covered stars.

Now.

With all her might, Fey swung out in front of her, landing a blow to Frankie's temple. For a brief moment, Frankie's laugh seeped out a little longer. Even in the pitch darkness, Fey thought she could see that one stray curl swing wildly in front of Frankie's face. She gave a second swing, aiming the same direction as before. She felt it land in the same place. A second *thud* and Frankie fell backward into the brush behind her. The disregarded flashlight rolled. Its bulb aimed upward, illuminating her face. In a few split seconds, Fey watched Frankie's smile fade and her eyes roll backward. Her mouth was agape and her eyes were left slightly open.

Fey's memory flashed to the day she identified Bruce through the photo on the coroner's desk. Frankie laying in front of her echoed the image burned in her brain. Her eyes were slits, as if she were drifting off to sleep. Her mouth hung open to the side as if she wanted to call out, but didn't have the energy. The only difference was that her temples were coated in bright red splatter. It hadn't had the time to congeal and darken. Underneath the pooling blood, Fey could see another difference. Frankie's head was no longer perfectly rounded. It caved in where her club had hit. It turned out, maybe Fey was stronger than Frankie after all.

Fey scrambled over Frankie's body and grabbed for the flashlight, afraid Frankie would get up at any moment to reprimand her. It was unlikely, but someone as evil as Frankie may need more than a crushed skull to stop her.

Gathering her breath and herself, Fey stood up on both legs. Now, armed with a light to lead her feet, she stepped forward. She left her trusted branch-crutch-shield-club discarded. She didn't need it anymore. She was, after all, strong. Strong enough to stand up for herself. Strong enough to simply stand. She no longer needed a crutch, neither made from a tree nor from fabricated friendship. One tiny step after another, she made her way toward freedom. For the first time in 21 years, Fey Anderson realized she could fully stand on her own.

CHAPTER TWENTY – FIVE

A wash of relief ran over Fey when she saw the first sign for the blue trail. She stepped on the dirt path, putting the overgrown brush behind her. She followed it, taking a thankful breath every time she saw another sign leading her to the parking lot.

But when she reached the parking lot, she stood still. There was the empty golden Beetle, waiting for Frankie to take the driver's seat. And next to the car was a familiar figure with a shaggy haircut.

June.

Fey shuffled her feet, trying to decide her next move. Should she try running past as fast as her bad ankle would take her? Or should she take stealthy steps behind June's back, hoping to go undetected?

Wait, is June crying?

Fey could hear June sniffling into her hands. She found it hard to believe June's hard exterior had cracked enough for the emotion to seep out. She eased her steps toward the opposite side of the car, hoping to blend with the shadows.

Fey slipped on the gravel as she reached the passenger's side door. June's sniffling stopped and she turned around.

Shit!

Fey ducked for cover, but it was too late—June had already seen her.

"Frankie's gone."

June's statement rang through the air in finality and, suddenly, Fey didn't feel like running. She straightened herself up and nodded, wary of what to expect next.

"Frankie's. Gone," June repeated.

"Yeah." Again, Fey nodded. She cleared her throat, forcing her voice out. "Yeah, she's gone." Through the moonlight, Fey could see something she had never noticed in June's eyes before. "Say, June, you okay?"

June nodded back. Hope. Fey saw hope in June's eyes.

"You know, Frankie was right about something."

June furrowed her brow. She reached up to her mop hair, touching the short ends.

"No, not about your hair." Fey felt herself relax into the conversation. "Ally did a great job on it. It looks great on you. A lot better than what I have going on." Fey rolled her eyes up to indicate her own disheveled hair.

June eased her hands to her side.

"You seem pretty strong to me, June."

June furrowed her brows again.

"Not many people could walk out of this standing on their own two feet." Fey pointed to her own bad ankle and loosely chuckled. She stopped when she saw June's expression change again.

"Look, I don't know what thumb Frankie had you under, but she sure has done a number on you. You're not alone in that. Shit, June. She did a number on me, too. But I think maybe you were a little smarter than I was. You played her game well enough to keep yourself alive."

June's gaze fell to the gravel, and Fey felt the tension rise in the air again. Maybe she wasn't reading June correctly yet. It was possible June was just as invested in Frankie's vision as Frankie was. Fey bit her lip and reluctantly began to drag her feet out of the parking lot. She mentally prepared herself to make a run for it if she needed to.

"You too," June said to her back.

Fey turned around, surprised June was looking to hold a conversation.

"You kept yourself alive, too."

"I suppose I did."

Fey exhaled as she realized the tension was probably from June opening up in a way she never had before. She considered the walk she would need to take out on the main road and into town. It would be a couple of miles before she would reach anyone, possibly more. She looked up at the half moon above. Chances were, all of Soura were tucked within their homes, safely removed from the dangers of night.

Fey gave June a weakened smile and pointed to the V.W. "I suppose you don't have the ignition keys to that, do you?"

June looked thoughtfully at the car she was leaning against. She bit her bottom lip and furrowed her brow, then shrugged her shoulders. "Frankie has them."

"Ah. I see." Fey had been half-hopeful, half-grateful. Without a way to drive the car away, there would be no obvious way to tie Fey and June to it. To Tom Brickshaw, it would appear that Frankie drove herself to Covista and fell victim in the same way countless others did. He'd brush it off as an accident. Soura Heights would mourn the pie shop owner's passing and over time, they would appoint a new cornerstone to lean on.

Fey held her hand out and gestured for June to follow her. "Come on, June. Let's get out of here."

They allowed the silver moon to light their way out of the gravel parking lot and to the main road. As they fell into step, June allowed Fey to use her arm when the pain in her ankle became too much.

Every foot forward brought them away from Bruce's last breath and the mountain lion. Each step was one away from the traps that would eat them up. Together, they were putting Frankie behind the both of them and finding the strength within themselves to move forward.

"June, you doing okay over there?"

June nodded her head.

"You know, Frankie told me the story of the day she found you in a car accident." Fey's voice trailed off. Earlier this week, she would have been full of nerves to start a conversation with June, let alone ask her about a near-death experience. "Did she really save your life?"

June let out a sigh and pursed her lips. "Frankie pulled me from the car." When she spoke, it was like the words pulled out like

Velcro. They ripped little by little from her tongue to give a short, direct answer..

Fey nodded and leaned on June's arm for support. "Yeah, she said that. She also said she took you home and took care of you."

June stopped dead in her tracks and her eyes widened. Fey thought she saw them glisten with tears. "Frankie saved me." She then exhaled as if she were breathing out all the trauma she held onto since the day Frankie found her around that tree.

Fey nodded. Of course Frankie saved her. She saved her to have leverage. Fey pictured herself in June's shoes. Had Frankie saved her life, she would have worked herself to the bone repaying her. She imagined June felt the same and worked herself to the bone for Frankie's approval on everything.

Fey lightly pulled June's arm forward, urging her to continue toward Rosecourt. "You know, Ally did do a good job on your hair. It looks good on you."

June touched the ends of her shaggy cut and shrugged her shoulders. "Frankie didn't think so."

Now Fey stopped in her tracks. "She didn't, did she?"

It all made sense. June would have done anything for Frankie's approval, anything. She took over half the pie shop. She'd follow Frankie's instructions. She'd be Frankie's right hand in her plan to keep Soura the way it had always been. And when she didn't have her approval after her haircut, she needed to win it back somehow. What better way than to march back into the woods and ensure she had a hand in the last fallen job.

June took a step forward and pulled Fey's arm with her. Regardless of whose approval June was working for in the past, they were leaving it behind them.

They continued this way all the way back to Rosecourt. Their conversation was awkward, their gait clumsy. But for the first time since she moved away from Saint Paign, Fey felt like she was getting a real connection with another person.

EPILOGUE

"Thanks for letting me poke through some of these books," Fey called through a gap in one of the tall bookcases.

Miss Davis grunted from the front of the store. She had become more lenient in letting people flip through pages, as long as they walked away with a purchase under their arms.

Fey found a handful of cookbooks to sift through. She collected them on her lap in the corner on the floor and opened their pages. She was hoping to find one that had an easy-to-follow triple berry recipe.

The front doors chimed and Fey looked up from her spot. Claire walked in with BettyAnne skipping by her feet.

"Come on, Mom! Come on!" BettyAnne was pulling Claire's hand by the fingertips.

"Hold on, BettyAnne." Claire turned to Miss Davis. "Miss Davis, do you have any books on birds?"

Miss Davis threw her crooked finger in the air and waved it at the aisle next to where Fey was sitting.

"Thank you, Miss Davis. Okay, BettyAnne, let's go have a look."

"Yay!" BettyAnne raced her mom over to the shelf as Miss Davis shushed her from her chair.

Claire knelt down to BettyAnne's level and spoke in a hushed voice, "Let's see what we have here…"

Fey watched as a few books went missing from the shelf and Claire's eyes peeked through.

"Oh, hi Fey!"

Miss Davis shushed again.

Claire lowered her voice. "What are you doing here?"

"Just some research." Fey held up a book with an oven on the cover.

"Ah, I see. You'll have everything running smooth as butter before you know it. No doubt, Frankie left some secret recipe cards somewhere." Even though her voice held a chipper timbre, her eyes sank into sadness.

Fey gave a meek smile. "I'm sure she was full of all kinds of secrets."

"Mommy! This looks just right!" Fey could see the top of a book BettyAnne was holding up.

"It sure does, BettyAnne. Say, Fey," Claire peeked through the hole in the bookstack again, "do you know anything about birds?"

Shit. This again?

Fey shook her head.

Claire and BettyAnne walked around to the same side of the bookcase. BettyAnne held up the book she chose. "There's a nest in the bush in our front yard and it had five eggs in it! Three have hatched, but one of the birds is missing."

Claire put her hand over her mouth to whisper, "Something ate it, but I don't know what." She had the same fear in her eyes when they were dealing with Patches.

BettyAnne's eyes grew wide and watery. Fey clenched her jaw, anticipating she was going to cry over the baby bird's death. Instead, BettyAnne handed the book to Claire and ran over to kneel on the floor next to Fey. With wide eyes, she threw her arms around Fey's neck.

Fey held her breath, not daring to move from the spot.

BettyAnne let go. "It felt like you needed that." She wiped her eyes and grabbed the book from Claire. "Okay, Mom, let's go home!"

"Not yet, miss. I still have work to do. But you can bring that book and look at the pictures in the backroom if you'd like."

BettyAnne grumbled, but took her mother's hand as they paid and left the store.

Fey flipped through the top book in her hands. After a few minutes, she found what she needed and decided to buy the whole stack anyway. After all, customers anticipated a new flavor every week.

Fey hugged her books as her feet clicked against the cobblestone. Katrina waved from the window of the nail salon, and Fey nodded as she walked by. The display window at Tell Me Wear caught her attention. The mannequins were positioned the same, but their clothing had changed. Now, they all wore denim pants and button-down plaid shirts.

Taking a deep breath, Fey took a moment to reflect on who Richard Teft may have been. A truck driver with a slow route? A retail builder scouting out new lots of land? A lumberjack hoping to land new work in the forest? No one would know.

A familiar hand touched Fey's shoulder, breaking her away from contemplation.

"Oh, hi Louise."

"The star birds!" Louise raised her hands up to the sky, waving her fingers in wide circles. "They're satisfied and happy with their meals wrapped in fur. They're singing their common songs of happiness and joy. It's so good to dance to it."

Then, she leaned in close to Fey and whispered, "And the red foxes finished serving their bittery meals, haven't they?"

Fey nodded her head as if she understood. Something caught her peripheral attention behind Louise's head. There, in the sky, two large vultures made passes in the air, laying claim. Somewhere down the road, there must have been a roadkill meal waiting for them. Their black figures circled around and around, and for the first time, Fey noticed their feathered markings. With their wings out, their feathered tips splayed into several white points.

White stars.

Louise's eyes grew wide and her smile revealed a missing back tooth Fey never noticed before. "The lynx might hide from her hero-doing, but I see her. She didn't fall for the fox's tricks anymore. The star birds are happy to have their normal foods again. No more sour meals full of bitterness and melancholy. They're done with their songs and the Todds and Vixens are finished, too." She leaned in close to whisper again, "Jonny says no one needs to be fallen again." Louise clapped her hands and dance-walked in a circle. A little bit of the life Fey saw in the living room photo had returned to the current Louise.

Fey chimed through Pie-Pie For Now's doors, and June welcomed her with a smile.

I could get used to that.

Fey brought the books to the backroom and sat them down on a shelf near the oven. She opened the oven door and breathed in the sweet scent that emitted from inside. "Strawberry rhubarb smells done!" she called out to the front room. Fey grabbed a pair of oven mitts and pulled it out, letting it cool on an empty burner. She grabbed an apron from the backroom and pulled it over her head.

When she walked through the swinging doors, she saw June leave a table where Tom and Peggy Brickshaw were seated and make her way to the shelves of pies.

"Is Tom looking for a pie of the week?"

June nodded, her eyes low. "There is none."

"That's okay, June. I'll take care of it." Fey grabbed a key lime and placed it on the top shelf under the **Pie of the Week** label.

She brought a slice over to the table. "Here you are, Tom, Peggy. One slice, two forks." She pointed to a small jar of honey in the middle of the table. "Feel free to dress it up if you'd like. A little bit of honey is my personal favorite."

Peggy gave Fey a sympathetic smile, her eyes holding a tender sadness Fey was supposed to feel.

Tom tapped the table with his finger. "Thank you, Fey. Listen-" He scratched the back of his neck. "I just wanted to extend my sincere condolences. I know you were close to Frankie and for her to go like that, it's...it's just a shame."

Fey motioned a hand for him to stop. His condolences weren't needed.

"The whole town has lost someone special, haven't they? She was well loved, always brought our close knit community even closer." Tom's hands moved to the top of the table. He drummed his fingers. "I guess it just goes to show you that even someone who knows Covista well can be-"

"Eaten up by the forest?" Fey chimed in.

Tom nodded. "Yeah, I guess so. Funny how that happens, isn't it? Well, not funny... but... you know what I mean." He gave a quick, nervous laugh. "Anyway, I'm just sorry you have to go through this again. It's just a shame."

Fey would let Tom believe his legend of the hungry forest. Involving him any further than that wasn't worth it. His blind sympathy was his sole value to Soura Heights. It gave the town a sense of peace to have someone with a caring tone as their authority figure. No, Fey wouldn't divulge the details to him. She was stronger than that. Strong enough to handle things in her way. Strong enough to keep the Soura Heights community the way it should be, in her image.

Fey's peripheral vision alerted her to someone else, someone new. A man in his 20s wearing a black band t-shirt and a matching baseball cap. Shaggy brown hair peeked out from under the cap, and a square faced watch adorned his left wrist. She appreciated the proof that some people still use watch faces to tell the time rather than relying on their phones. He was standing by the entrance, surveying the front display with the glass tea canisters. Fey thought she saw him chuckle at the Pie-Pie For Now logo. Good, he had a sense of humor this town would appreciate. Clearly a fish out of water, he looked around the diner with wide eyes.

Instinctively, Fey stole another look at June. There was a malicious twinkle in her eye, as if she were invited to play a childhood game and knew a loophole that always brought her the win.

Damn it, Frankie. You still have a hold on her.

Fey imagined this man's story. His casual dress told her he wasn't traveling through on business. Concentrating on his shirt, she realized it wasn't a band she had ever heard of. More than likely, it was a small-town indie band full of softly sung poetic melodies. Maybe he was following them on a lowkey tour from one hole-in-the-wall bar to another, hoping to make a name for themselves in one of the bigger cities. Their next stop may as well be in Saint Paign. Perhaps they would find themselves at the same bar she and Bruce used to pass by, full of bass-driven music and dark scenery lit up by glow-in-the-dark bracelets and black lights. His name was probably something like Raine or Duncan, and he was young enough to live off roadside adrenaline and stops for pie.

Raine (or Duncan) invited himself to a booth with a menu in his hand. Even though he held the menu up, his eyes were searching the pie racks. June's hands twitched nervously as she adjusted her apron and Fey could see the confidence slowly creep up in her as she made her way to Duncan (or Raine). She pictured June introducing herself, stiffly holding out her hand. At first she would struggle getting a conversation going, but as her goal became clearer, she would ease into chatter that would make him uncomfortable.

Fey intercepted June at the front counter. "Here, June." She handed her a watering can hidden on a shelf behind the counter. "Will you take this over to Fern and give it a little water?"

June nodded. She blinked and relief ran over her body as she took the watering can from Fey. Fern took the place where the Covista trap had lived. Fey felt safe with Fern around, like Fern was keeping a watchful eye out, protecting her when needed. She knew Fern would look after June as well.

Smiling, Fey approached Raine (or Duncan). As she got closer, she realized he was a little older than she first guessed. The bags under his eyes were from more than nights full of loud music and no sleep. The tell-tale wrinkles by the corners of his eyes added to the telling of his age. Within his dark shaggy hair, there were a few silver strands that also peeked out from under his hat. It was more likely he was aging into his late 30s or older. Oddly, he tapped his watch and she realized that it wasn't a sleek Alpina or Seiko she had assumed. No, this watch had a touchscreen surface, a tiny computer that simply fit around his wrist. He wasn't the carefree kid who enjoyed life's simple pleasures like she had thought.

Fey took her phone out of her pocket and set herself a reminder: *Google smart watches.*

"Welcome to Pie-Pie For Now!" Fey slipped her phone back in place, put on her most charming voice, and drew a chair up to the table. She'd take his order and listen.

She wouldn't imagine or picture his story in her head. She would ask for it directly from him. She'd dig into who he really was and befriend him within minutes. She'd let him open up to her and give her details about his life, about the tour he was following or the roadside stops he's taken. She'd let him talk openly about how he would improve the small-town life in Soura Heights, how a new corner bar with space for live music would be great for both the community and his ambitious indie band. She'd give him her full attention without the same judgment Frankie had and allow June to watch from the sidelines. There wouldn't be any verbal Velcro to pull. She would be comfortable and at ease. She'd get to know him and then decide how the story of Soura Heights should go—safe, for everyone. That included Raine/Duncan/Joe and anyone else who dropped into Soura's scenery. She'd write Soura's story in her image, in her Wonderland, as long as she was strong enough.

A REVIEW REQUEST

I cannot thank you enough for spending some of your time reading this book! Independently published books are ridiculously hard to get noticed. If you made it this far, please consider leaving a review on Amazon and/or Goodreads. Every review is incredibly helpful.

Thank you!

ACKNOWLEDGEMENTS

2020 gave us all the gift of time. (At least, that's how I choose to see it.) I'm so glad it did because it caused me to finally sit down and put the story that's been swarming in my head on paper. However, if it weren't for a great team of people, it would have never turned into the fully envisioned story it is today.

First and foremost, I want to thank my husband for being my rock. Your support through this learning process has given me the stability I needed to bring my dream into reality.

My kids. Girls, may you become the strong women I know you're destined to be. Also, I'm sorry for the many times you asked, "Mommy, what are you writing?" and I've had to dilute it down. One day, you'll be able to safely read it when you're older. (Even though, I know you've snuck your own peeks when I wasn't looking.)

To my parents and extended family: thank you for your support. Even without diving into this story before its published date, you've rooted for its success. I'll forever be thankful for you being my lifeline cheerleaders.

My alphas and betas: Steve, Rob, Douglas, Emily, and Tracy. Without you, my story would have been stuck in the boring infant stages. I appreciate all the constructive criticism you gave to round it out the way it needed to be.

Thank you to Troy Cooper, who designed my cover when I was so unsure of what it should be.

Thank you to Genevieve Scholl, "Editor Eve," for tidying up everything in a presentable bow and making sure nothing slides through the cracks.

And my readers. Thank you for reading and taking a chance on me and my work. Your time is valuable and the fact you chose to spend some of it on little 'ol me fills me up with more gratitude than you'll ever know.

ABOUT THE AUTHOR

Amanda Jaeger has always had an interest in true crime, suspense, and mystery. As a long term copywriter, she has always had a hand in writing creatively for businesses to boost their income.
She's the wife of her college sweetheart, and the mother of two spit-fire girls, but she's also been a sign language interpreter, transcriptionist, and a book slinger. Working with words isn't her job, it's her career.

Now, she uses her knowledge and experience in engaging an audience and applies it into her author career, crafting suspense and mystery to keep readers on the edge of their seats.
Residing in Virginia, you can bet on Amanda listening to true crime podcasts, watching cold case documentaries, and playing with her kids. (Not simultaneously).

"What do you do with an English degree?"
"You write." -Amanda Jaeger

You can connect with Amand on social media:
Facebook: @AmandaJaegerAuthor
Instagram: @Amanda.B.Jaeger

Printed in Great Britain
by Amazon

64940817R00123